HAUNTED DARLINGTON

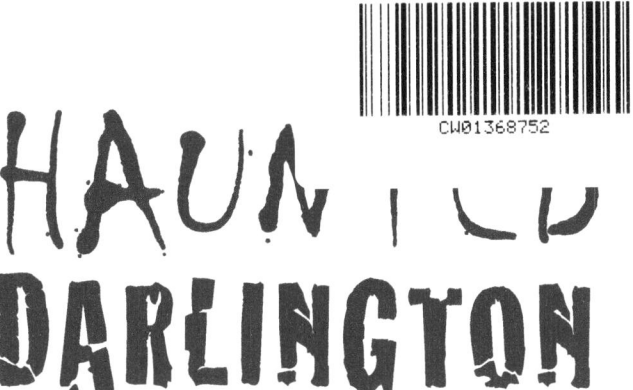

HAUNTED DARLINGTON

Robert Woodhouse

First published 2015

The History Press
The Mill, Brimscombe Port
Stroud, Gloucestershire, GL5 2QG
www.thehistorypress.co.uk

© Robert Woodhouse, 2015

The right of Robert Woodhouse to be identified as the Author
of this work has been asserted in accordance with the
Copyright, Designs and Patents Act 1988.

All rights reserved. No part of this book may be reprinted
or reproduced or utilised in any form or by any electronic,
mechanical or other means, now known or hereafter invented,
including photocopying and recording, or in any information
storage or retrieval system, without the permission in writing
from the Publishers.

British Library Cataloguing in Publication Data.
A catalogue record for this book is available from the British Library.

ISBN 978 0 7524 6991 1

Typesetting and origination by The History Press
Printed in Great Britain

CONTENTS

	Acknowledgements	6
	Introduction	7
one	Aquatic Horrors for Early Inhabitants	19
two	Spooks on the Roads To and From Darlington	22
three	Spooky Residential Areas	40
four	Haunted Town Centre Locations	48
five	Ghostly Animals	65
six	Supernatural Sightings on the Industrial Front	69
seven	Ghoulish Goings-on at School	73
eight	Supernatural Incidents at Durham Tees Valley Airport	75
nine	Supernatural Locations Just Beyond Darlington	79
ten	Ghost Hunting in Times Past	88
	Epilogue	90
	About the Author	92
	Select Bibliography	93

ACKNOWLEDGEMENTS

A long-standing interest in aspects of history relating to north-east England has uncovered countless reports of supernatural activity. Many of these episodes were highlighted in local newspapers, almanacs and wide-ranging reference works, but others have been supplied by friends, relatives and members of the public and I am extremely grateful to all the individuals and organisations who have provided such material.

Photographs are from my own collection apart from those on pages 9, 11, 14, 16, 18, 23, 44, 49, 51, 52 and 54–57, which were provided by Beamish Regional Resource Centre.

The locations covered are either within Darlington Borough Council district or form part of neighbouring areas. In particular I am indebted to staff at Darlington Central Reference Library for their invaluable assistance in tracing material in newspapers and an assortment of reference works, and to members of my local history classes on 'Supernatural North Country' for contributing additional features. A final word of thanks is due to Liz Taylorson for her typing and administrative work.

INTRODUCTION

It does seem quite strange that some places in the North of England appear to have more ghostly locations than other settlements of a similar size in different parts of the country. Perhaps this is because places like York, Durham and Newcastle on Tyne have such a long history of human occupation that there are simply more restless souls who have yet to find peace. On the other hand, Darlington is rather smaller in size, with less evidence of early human activity, yet it can boast a whole range of supernatural sightings. Maybe Darlington's residents are simply more conscious, aware or perceptive when it comes to paranormal activity …

Northern folk certainly seem to be at the forefront when it comes to ghostly credentials, for a recent National Opinion Poll concluded that six out of ten people in the region claimed to have felt the presence of a ghost. These figures far outweighed numbers calculated for the Midlands and the South of England.

Down the centuries, ghostly characters and paranormal themes have regularly featured in literary works but the whole question of ghosts, phantoms, apparitions (or whatever term is applied)

Darlington coat of arms.

only started to gain widespread publicity in Britain during the seventeenth century. This rapid growth of interest was certainly due, at least in part, to an increase in accusations of witchcraft and the activities of the 'Witch-finder

General'. In more recent times the subject of ghost hunting has gained an amount of academic credibility and committed groups of researchers employ a range of technical devices during their rigorous investigations.

Of course there is also research to rationalise paranormal findings and scientific analysis examines the psychological and medical evidence behind supernatural sightings. For example, findings reported by researchers at Edinburgh University in the later weeks of 2011 concluded that near-death experiences are not paranormal but stimulated by a normal change in brain function, while the effects of noradrenaline – a hormone released by the brain – are known to fuel hallucinations. Many ghostly occurrences can undoubtedly be explained away as tricks of our own imagination but with such a range of sightings by people from all sorts of backgrounds, it is perhaps difficult to dismiss all such reports as entirely delusional.

If spectral sightings are linked to events or incidents connected with the full range of human activity in the past then the region covered by Darlington and neighbouring areas has an extremely varied and impressive range of settings, both urban and rural, within its boundaries.

Although the first documentary evidence of a settlement at 'Dearthingtun' only appears in an eleventh-century land grant, experts suggest that an Anglian community existed close to the cemetery that was uncovered on the Greenbank estate in 1876 and the discovery of fragments of ninth- or tenth-century crosses in St Cuthbert's church point to an earlier church building on the west side of the present building.

The Bishop of Durham's manor house was probably built in the 1160s on a site to the south of the churchyard and by the mid-thirteenth century, Darlington market and annual fairs attracted large numbers of people from most areas of the north-east.

By the late fourteenth century the town was playing an important part in the shipment of wool to the Continent and clearly defined routes through the town had also been established with streets such as Houndgate, Blackwellgate, Skinnergate and Northgate most prominent.

A long line of academic institutions in the town may well have begun with an early grammar school linked with the collegiate church of St Cuthbert. Following the opening of another grammar school and a chantry chapel in 1530, Queen Elizabeth I granted a charter for the establishment of a further grammar school during 1563. Design work for Victorian grammar school buildings and several of the town's other notable properties, including Elm Ridge on Carmel Road South, was carried out by George Gordon Hoskins (1837–1911) who was based in Russell Street Buildings, Northgate, from 1864.

Darlington's growth as an industrial and commercial centre during the second half of the nineteenth century highlighted the need for improved medical facilities and in 1865 the town's first public hospital opened in Russell Street. The grey brickwork of new hospital buildings in Greenbank Road took shape between 1883–85 but during the interwar years the focus of medical care shifted to a site on Hollyhurst Road with construction of the Memorial Hospital. This site was officially opened on Friday, 5 May 1933 by HRH Prince George, KG, GCVO.

Darlington Grammar School, built in 1874–77 to designs by G.G. Hoskins..

Darlington's first public hospital (opened in 1865).

A great deal of the impetus for Darlington's economic growth was provided by Quaker families who began to settle in the town during the 1660s. Woollen and linen industries became increasingly centralised in their hands and, following a rise in population to over 4,500 by 1801, the next fifty years saw a further increase to more than 12,000.

Much of this demographic activity resulted from the opening of the Stockton and Darlington Railway in September 1825 and the leading figure in this venture was one of the town's foremost Quaker citizens, Edward Pease.

The railway not only improved Darlington's trading links but also stimulated associated industries including locomotive, carriage and wagon building as well as production of raw materials such as iron and steel. By 1867 there were three blast furnaces, 153 puddling furnaces and nine finishing mills in the town.

The influence of Quaker families such as Pease and Backhouse spread far beyond railways and may be found in many parts of the town. On the north side of Houndgate – close to the market place – is Pease's House, birthplace of Edward Pease, while Northgate Lodge, a bow-fronted house dating from 1830, was at one time the home of John Beaumont Pease (a nephew of Edward Pease).

Many of Darlington's imposing buildings were designed by Sir Alfred Waterhouse and these include the old town hall (opened in 1864) along with the market hall and clock tower, which was a gift to the town from Joseph Pease. A short distance away, towards the northern end of High Row, Barclays Bank – formerly

Graveyard and walls of the Friends Meeting House in Skinnergate.

View of Darlington from the top of Pease's Mill in 1938, between Tubwell Row and Priestgate.

Mechanics' Institute on Skinnergate.

Backhouse's Bank – was designed by Waterhouse in the Victorian Gothic style and was also completed in 1864.

Several of the town's other nineteenth-century buildings were designed by J.P. Pritchett and among them are the Mechanics' Institute on Skinnergate, which dates from 1853. Skinnergate also has several examples of Darlington's 'yards', which formerly housed workers and their families. On the east side, between Skinnergate and High Row, are Mechanic's Yard, Clark's Yard and Buckton's Yard, while on the opposite side is Friends' Yard.

During the last decades of the nineteenth century, Darlington gained other distinctive buildings, including the library in Crown Street and the original Technical College building on Northgate. Edward Pease (1834–1880) provided finance for the library that opened in 1885 and on the roadside there is an intriguing link with a former editor of the *Northern Echo*, W.T. Stead. A small boulder with attached metal ring was used by the newspaper chief to tether his pony after travelling to his nearby office from the family home at Grainey Hill Cottage, Hummersknott.

The town's first Technical College building, located in Northgate, was opened by the Duke of Devonshire in 1897. In front of the premises stands a large glacial boulder known as Bulmer Stone, which takes its name either from the Bulmer family who owned adjacent property or from a town crier, Willie Bulmer, who is reported to have stood on the stone to read news items to the townsfolk.

Darlington Free Library on Crown Street, built in 1884–85.

Hitching Stone outside Darlington Library.

Northgate pictured in 1910.

The Bulmer Stone c. 1890

This boulder of Shap granite was left here by the last Ice Age circa 10,000 B.C. Other erratics are scattered over the North East. At one time the stone marked the northern boundary of the town. It got its name from Willy Bulmer, Borough Crier, in the early nineteenth century, who called out the London news when it arrived by stage – coach.

At one time it was known as the "Battling Stone", as the town weavers used to beat their flax on it.

An information panel for the Bulmer Stone, Darlington's oldest landmark.

The Bulmer Stone, Northgate.

North Road, Darlington. This photograph was taken around the 1920s.

New Hippodrome Theatre, Parkgate, now renamed Darlington Civic Theatre (opened in 1907 and photographed around this time).

While the late eighteenth century saw the opening of theatres in nearby townships such as Stockton-on-Tees (in 1766) and Richmond (1788), the influence of Darlington's Quaker citizens probably inhibited similar developments in the town. During the early 1800s, Thorn's Theatre was set up in Clay Row before moving to premises in Blackwellgate and several other theatrical ventures were short-lived before the opening of the Hippodrome in Parkgate on 2 September 1907.

During the early years, management was in the hands of Signor Rino Pepi, an Italian who gave up a stage career to concentrate on running theatrical venues in the north-east, and an array of star performers appeared on the Hippodrome's stage. Rino Pepi died on 17 November 1927, hours before a performance by the legendary ballerina, Pavlova, and by this time the theatre was suffering severe financial difficulties. A local syndicate of businessmen bought the building for £18,500 but the 1930s saw more financial crises and regular changes in management. After a short period of closure the theatre was reopened by Darlington Amateur Operatic Society in 1958 and, following a major programme of cleaning and refurbishment, the society's production of *White Horse Inn* was a major success.

Few productions were staged over the next few years and, although the building was purchased by Darlington Corporation for £8,000 in 1964 (with full control two years later) after which further improvements were made, the theatre's fortunes remained at a low ebb. A dramatic turning point came in 1972 following the appointment of Peter Tod as theatre director and within five years he had increased audiences from 20 per cent of capacity to almost 85 per cent. The theatre's 80th anniversary was marked with the news that average attendances of 95 per cent represented the highest audiences of any provincial theatre and schemes to refurbish the interior and increase seating capacity have ensured that Darlington Civic Theatre maintains its place as one of the country's foremost provincial theatres.

During the Edwardian period, housing development had spread almost as far as Cockerton and the village was incorporated in 1915, while on the eastern side of the town, Haughton-le-Skerne was added in 1930. During successive phases of industrial expansion, Darlington maintained its position as the market centre for a large agricultural hinterland and this has been reflected in schemes to remodel the town's market place and adjacent areas.

Just beyond the south-eastern corner of the market place is the new town hall. Built on the site of the Bishop of Durham's manor house (which was demolished in 1970), it was designed by Williamson and Faulkner Brown of Newcastle on Tyne in conjunction with the borough architect, and officially opened by HRH Princess Anne on 27 May 1970. Other recent town centre schemes that reflect Darlington's continued prosperity include the Dolphin Centre, a large sporting and leisure complex on the southern side of the market place, and the Cornmill Shopping Centre, which covers a large area of ground between Tubwell Row, Northgate and Crown Street.

Another chapter in the town's municipal history opened on 1 April 1997 when Darlington became a unitary authority. Within a wider context the Borough of Darlington includes not only the township of Darlington but also surrounding rural areas containing twenty-six civil parishes ranging from Heighington on the northern edge to Hurworth on the southern flank. It is from this area of the Borough of Darlington and the surrounding neighbourhood that assorted tales, incidents and episodes of a supernatural nature have been gathered to comprise *Haunted Darlington*.

Miss Joyce Banks (left) and a colleague taking part in Our Miss Gibbs *performed by Darlington Operatic Society in 1935.*

ONE

AQUATIC HORRORS FOR EARLY INHABITANTS

Three watercourses have played a major role in defining Darlington's geographical setting and in shaping the lifestyle of early settlers in the area. The rivers Tees and Skerne, along with the Cocker Beck, not only formed natural boundaries but also supplied water for domestic and industrial use as well as being a transport route. Place name experts suggest that early variations of the town's name, such as 'Darningtun' or 'Dearthington', were based on 'dare' meaning water, 'ing' a meadow and 'ton' a settlement, which together indicate the township on the watery meadows.

Yet all too often the river's measured flow could rapidly and dramatically change into a swirling, gushing torrent that carried away livestock, buildings and unwary humans. Little wonder then that any number of riverside tales were passed on from generation to generation and many of these featured the 'Headless Hobgoblin' of Neasham.

Most sightings were reported along the stretch of riverside roadway between Hurworth and Neasham but, because of a measure of physical deformity, this strange spectre was unable to cross the small stream that drained into the Tees at Neasham. Descriptions varied – often distorted by the hours of darkness and extreme weather conditions – but the hob was generally regarded as a kelpie, an evil spirit that lurked beside the river before luring men, women and children into the watery depths. Inevitably, in each reported case, water levels rose and victims were drowned until matters came to a dramatic conclusion on 31 December 1722.

Robert Luck, a Darlington bricklayer, was said to have had the misfortune to come across the Hob on the roadway between Hurworth and Neasham. Like so many other unfortunate travellers, Robert disappeared into the depths of the nearby Tees leaving local villagers so upset and outraged that they planned immediate decisive action. The hated Hob was exorcised and buried under a large roadside stone with a warning that anyone who sat on the stone would be glued there indefinitely.

No doubt there was a great deal of foreboding when the road was rebuilt at the end of the nineteenth century for this work involved disturbing, and then removing, the resting place of Neasham's Headless Hobgoblin. Thankfully though, since that time there have been no further reports of this fearsome presence.

Foaming Clues to a Freshwater Mermaid

As fears of the 'Headless Hobgoblin' subsided so talk among local folk focused on Peg Powler, a ghostly freshwater mermaid. Perhaps it was a growth in population levels during the seventeenth century that led to frightening tales designed to deter small children from the banks of the Tees.

Secretive and mysterious, Peg Powler was never to be seen; her presence was supposedly indicated by the presence of clouds of foam left behind when she washed her distinctive green hair. Youngsters knew that those dangerous waters of the Tees were to be avoided at all costs.

Spectral Images from the River Skerne

Local newspapers of the 1930s often included reports of ghostly sightings such as the account in April 1938 of a house (unnamed) where residents heard the sound of someone walking in rustling silks. Other sounds included the breaking of invisible sticks or trailing imperceptible chains along the floor, and the ghost was said to indulge in a range of other terrifying tricks.

It was seen in the shape of a well-dressed man emerging from the River Skerne before setting his back against the house door and then vanishing. A tenant at the property did not stay long because of the reputed visits of the ghost, which was claimed to be the spirit of a man who was murdered in the house some twenty years before.

Military Man's Watery Plunge

An edition of the *Northern Despatch* in the early days of July 1932 carried reports of the ghost of a soldier who walked through Darlington town centre late at night before standing on a bridge over the River Skerne. As humans approached the apparition it is said to have leapt over the parapet, gurgling horribly as it fell into the river below with a terrible splash.

The River Skerne.

TWO

SPOOKS ON THE ROADS TO AND FROM DARLINGTON

DARLINGTON'S importance as a market centre ensured that a network of routes offered easy access to the town for traders and customers alike. But there was always the possibility of unnatural or even supernatural occurrences along the way.

Close to the busy route from the south via Croft (the modern A167 road) lie four strange ponds with the collective name of 'Hells Kettles', the largest of which measures 100ft in diameter. Their origins are unclear but according to local folklore they appeared on Christmas Day 1179 when the ground rose to a tremendous height and then fell 'with an horrible noise'. It is claimed that several people died of fright that day and since then strange happenings have been reported from the area of the pools at this location, which is now known as Oxen-le-Fields. Sounds of screaming and the neighing of horses are said to be linked with a local farmer who defied tradition by taking a load of hay to Darlington Market on 11 June (St Barnabas' Day), which is traditionally a day of rest. He is supposed to have disappeared as he passed the pools, snatched by the Devil because of his impiety. Perhaps this explains the belief among some of our ancestors that the ponds contain the souls of sinners and that these people (and in some cases, animals) can be seen floating in the pools when the surface water is clear.

Geologists offer a rational explanation for the formation of the pools by suggesting that a build-up of gases and water in large cavities within the magnesium limestone gradually worked through to the surface. Frogmen also disproved long-standing myths which stated that the pools were bottomless and found that the deepest one was only 20ft deep. Perhaps, then, the haunting sounds are actually caused by escaping gas and gurgling water, but who knows?

Phantom of a Celebrated Stockbreeder

On the north-east side of Darlington the hamlet of Barmpton became famous in stockbreeding circles during the early nineteenth century because of the work of the Colling brothers. Robert and Charles lived at Barmpton and Ketton halls and became pioneering breeders of the Durham ox. The brothers hired out their bulls for a year at a time in order to improve the quality of other herds at an annual fee of between 50 and 100 guineas. One particularly fine specimen was exhibited throughout England and Scotland between 1801 and 1807, drawing appreciative crowds at each venue. A special carriage was constructed to transport the huge ox from place to place but on 18 February 1807 disaster struck during a visit to Oxford. The ox slipped and dislocated its hip bone. When there was no improvement in its condition the beast had to be slaughtered on 15 April. It was 11 years old and weighed an incredible 270 stones.

Throughout the area no fewer than seventeen public houses were named after this legendary beast and these include The Comet at Hurworth Place, close to the northern end of Croft Bridge. Back at Barmpton, the hamlet's resident ghost was said to be that of Robert Colling who died on 8 March 1820 at the age of 73. After his death, regular sightings of this ghostly figure were made in the mornings, through a window of the hall, as he shaved himself.

Colling Shorthorn Memorial Challenge Cup.

Barmpton Hall, built in the late 1700s.

A more modern view of Barmpton Hall.

River Skerne near Barmpton.

Cat Kill Lane near Barmpton is rather overgrown.

River Skerne near Foxhill (north of Barmpton).

Kelton Hall, built in the late seventeenth century.

Haunting Spectre at the Baydale Beck Inn

During the seventeenth century, Darlington's suburbs were said to be frequented by highwaymen and lawless characters. Although those turbulent days have been replaced by calmer times, there are echoes of dramatic episodes at some of the landmark buildings.

Beside the west-bound A67 the Baydale Beck Inn is a popular modern hostelry but during the mid-eighteenth century it was a very different story. According to contemporary reports, the inn was used as a base by a notorious band of thieves known as Catton's gang, and by Sir William Browne, Knight of the Order of St Nicholas, along with his followers.

Browne's escapades were serious enough to warrant a sentence of death at Newcastle in 1743 after returning from transportation, and from this time reports were made of hauntings in and around this building. Ghostly visitations only added to this location's reputation for mystery and misdeeds – perhaps fostered by the lawbreakers' wish to avoid prying eyes.

Baydale Beck Inn.

Phantom Coach near Piercebridge

A copy of the *Darlington and Stockton Times* in November 1938 reported that during one afternoon in January 1880 two young girls were walking along the road near Piercebridge when they heard the sound of wheels behind them. Melting snow had turned the road surface into a messy state and the pair of friends stood well back to avoid being splashed. As the wheeled carriage passed, the girls glanced across and their interest soon turned to amazement. It was totally different from any vehicle that they had ever seen – with 'C' type springs at the rear and drawn by a pair of horses driven by a coachman. The mystery deepened as the girls thought they caught sight of a woman inside. Although they knew everyone in the neighbourhood they had no inkling about the identity of the woman or her speeding carriage.

Several years later the pair happened to be walking in the same area at about the same time when the mysterious vehicle reappeared. Their repeat sighting of the carriage soon became the main topic of conversation in Piercebridge and older folk then recalled similar incidents. They also spoke of an unseen carriage travelling further west to Stubb House where it stopped briefly at the front door before turning back.

Piercebridge village green with St Mary's church (opened 1873). This photograph was taken in 1905.

Spectral Female at Dyance Farm

Recent buildings at Dyance Farm, near Piercebridge, replaced a much older property on the site that featured in a fascinating tale from the late eighteenth century. In those days, travelling tailors made their way from house to house doing whatever work was required by the owners. One tailor found employment at the Dyance Farm property and, as he sat working, the ghostly figure of a woman would appear at the top of the stairs and throw down hanks of thread for him to use.

For many years there was no clue as to the identity of the spectre, with only vague references to 'a woman who had done something evil' among local folk, but then a chance discovery of documents at the Public Record Office threw a fresh and sinister light on events. It became clear that a woman named Catherine Hilton, who lived in the old house at Dyance in the reign of Queen Elizabeth I, had been accused of murdering a servant. Perhaps she sought to rectify her past misdeeds by helping the living in whatever small ways she could.

The George Hotel, Piercebridge.

George Hotel's Spectral Timepiece and a Female Phantom

Nowadays the village of Piercebridge has an atmosphere of peace and calm that belies turbulent episodes over the last 2,000 years. These included the establishment of a major Roman supply base and a savage encounter between Royalist and Roundhead forces in the later days of 1642, but it is the George Hotel, on the southern bank of the Tees, that is the focus for supernatural episodes.

A grandfather clock standing in a prominent position at the hotel was made by James Thompson whose business was based on Darlington's High Row during the early nineteenth century. The imposing timepiece was immortalised in the ballad *My Grandfather's Clock* because of its uncanny link with a former landlord, Christopher Charge.

Along with his wife, Christopher Charge spent the final years of his life at the George Hotel where the old clock was placed in one of their main rooms.

Ill health meant that he was confined to bed, and so the clock was moved into his bedroom and stationed at the bottom of his bed. When it was time for winding, Christopher – though now unable to speak because of his illness – would point to the clock, but soon after his death it stopped and, despite serious efforts, it could not be restarted.

The ballad that perpetuates this intriguing tale of a haunted clock was written by an American, Henry Clay Work, who overheard the landlord discussing details during a train journey from Newcastle.

Much less well known than the events surrounding 'My Grandfather's Clock' at the George Hotel is a tale connected with room 11. As is the case with most ghostly episodes, it involved tragic events linked to an uncanny apparition – in this case a beautiful young woman dressed in white. She was the daughter of one of the early landlords of the inn where the notorious highwayman, Dick Turpin, is said to have hidden away from pursuing forces of law.

Sadly, it seems that the young woman was crossed in love and, in a heartbroken state of mind; she hanged herself from a beam in room 11 of the inn. Her ghostly apparition is said to appear in fleeting form during the season of spring but only, it seems, if a young man is lodging in the upper room. Reports indicate that she approaches him stealthily before gently and tenderly resting her hand on his shoulder. Perhaps she is still desperately hoping for the return of her lover.

Walworth Castle's Ghostly Visitations

Walworth may be one of the north-east's lesser-known castles but it does have a fascinating mixture of architectural features and links, through previous owners, with a range of eminent personalities. Little wonder then that its welcoming rooms and staircases have also provided a number of intriguing supernatural surprises.

A modern view of Walworth Castle Hotel.

Set in open countryside between the A68 and B6279 roads to the north-west of Darlington, initial building work was completed in the late twelfth century by Gilbert Hansard. Walworth remained in the ownership of the Hansard family for around 400 years until it was sold to the Ayscough family of Lincolnshire. By this time the medieval structure, which probably had four towers enclosing a central courtyard, was partially ruined and during the mid-sixteenth century it was acquired by Thomas Jennison, an auditor-general to Queen Elizabeth I.

The Jennisons retained the distinctive Norman south wing of the castle but rebuilt the east and west sections with a fine porch and bay windows. Thomas Jennison was fatally injured in a fall from his horse while foxhunting in 1596 but the Walworth household were able to entertain royalty on 14 April 1603 when James VI of Scotland made an overnight stay on his way to London for his coronation.

In 1759 Walworth Castle was bought by General Aylmer who rebuilt the north wing and refurbished the main rooms with attractive Georgian plasterwork. Tragedy struck the Walworth household again when descendants of General Aylmer were killed in a petroleum train explosion in North Wales but the family coat of arms, which features in the stained-glass Venetian window on the staircase, serves as a fitting reminder of the Aylmer's links with Walworth.

During the early twentieth century, tenants at Walworth Castle included Sir Edward Cassel, a close friend of Edward VII (who may well have stayed here) and Sir Alfred and Lady Palmer who were based at Walworth until 1935. The war years (1939–45) saw the castle utilised by the Durham Light Infantry as

Tower at Walworth Castle Hotel.

an officers' mess and headquarters with other troops and prisoners of war billeted in the grounds.

After the war the Aylmer family sold Walworth Castle to Durham County Council who operated it as a school for girls before it was sold in 1981 and refurbished as a privately owned hotel.

With such a varied history and an assortment of architectural features it is hardly surprising that Walworth has been linked with ghostly visitations. A secret tunnel is said to run for about three-quarters of a mile to Low Walworth Farm but most of the paranormal activity seems to focus on the Jennison Suite where guests and hotel staff have been aware of someone, or something, pulling at their clothes or hair.

Coat of arms and the motto that appears above the door at Walworth Castle Hotel.

The sound of footsteps has been heard on the line of the old stone staircase, which was removed some time ago, and sightings of a spectral 'Grey Lady' have been reported. This phantom woman has been observed in various places, usually around the Jennison Suite but also in the turret sitting room, and there are a number of different suggestions about her identity. Reports claim that either a former owner of the castle, or in some cases a stable lad, began a relationship with a servant girl who subsequently became pregnant, and in an effort to resolve the situation the unfortunate young woman was immured within the walls of this part of the building. Some visitors have seen this phantom female peering from the walls at male guests, perhaps in the hope that her lover has returned.

A more recent mystery came to light in September 2011 when the hotel manager, Surinder Singh, discovered a crumpled sheet of paper behind a shutter in the en suite bathroom of guest accommodation. It dated from 1938 and was written by a mother living at an address in Sherburn, County Durham, to her daughter who was named Susan and probably worked at the property when it was a private residence. Sadly there is no record of what the letter contained, if indeed the contents was still legible.

With such a chequered history, who knows how many secrets of a human and paranormal nature are yet to be revealed amid the enthralling surroundings of Walworth Castle?

Blackwell Grange Spectre

In recent times the imposing family home of the Allan family, Blackwell Grange, has been tastefully adapted as a modern luxury hotel. Surrounded by 15 acres of woodland and an adjacent golf course, the walls and corridors of this stately mansion have witnessed any amount of drama, suspense and intrigue since the first building was completed on the site of a medieval manor house.

Much of the brickwork dates from 1710 with later extensions and additions in 1717 and 1900 and most of the building's compelling tales stem from the early years of occupation. George Allan oversaw completion of the three-storeyed section of the east range in 1710 and his son, also George, was able to find the time and finance to indulge his interest in genealogy, heraldry and natural history. He built up a remarkable museum and library, which was enhanced by a printing press to communicate data to friends and correspondents. Some years later George's prized collection was acquired by the Newcastle Philosophical Society and became the nucleus of displays in the city's Hancock Museum.

Thrift and shrewd business dealings characterised early generations of the Allan family and, down the years, reports have persisted of male members, notably two Georges and two Jameses, stealthily moving along silent corridors and state rooms in a vain search for lost antique items.

In the mid-eighteenth century the estate was held by Dorothy (known as 'Dolly'), who was remembered as a quaint and gentle soul, and her sister, Ann, who was given the title of 'Good Miss Allan' on account of her benevolence and charitable deeds. By the time of Ann's death in 1785, her generosity was so widely appreciated that

Blackwell Grange Hotel.

the funeral procession is said to have extended from St Cuthbert's church in Darlington, back to Blackwell Grange itself. Throughout her lifetime, Miss Allan put out a daily bowl of pence, along with meat and drink, for the benefit of poor folk and, on the occasion of her funeral, reports indicate that a dole was given to between 9,000 and 10,000 people amounting to one shilling for each adult and sixpence for children.

However, it seems that Ann Allan's generous nature did not extend to her dealings with domestic staff. When one of her maids became pregnant by Miss Allan's favourite coachman, the erring couple were ordered to appear before the lady of the house. After a lengthy verbal reprimand they were dismissed from their employment. The young coachman was so consumed by guilt and anguish that he hanged himself from one of the high lime trees in the grounds of Blackwell Grange. His spectre is said to appear from time to time around the estate, still lamenting his fate.

The most compelling phantom linked with this fascinating location is the so-called 'Tartan Lady' who featured in a life-sized portrait that was displayed in the long corridor of the south wing. The portrait had been presented to George Allan by Prince William, Duke of Cumberland, as he journeyed south after violent events on Culloden Field, but the dramatic painting soon became an object of extreme dislike among household staff.

It assumed a much more alarming reputation during April 1821 when a cousin of the current owner paid a visit to Blackwell Grange. When Robert Hodgeson arrived from York, where he was based as a lieutenant in the Dragoon Guards, George Allan was making an unscheduled overseas visit but the soldier was accorded a warm welcome by domestic staff.

Later in the evening, after a lavish evening meal, Robert Hodgeson was shown to his room by a long-serving manservant named Fletcher. As he was about to enter the bedroom the soldier looked back along the corridor and, spotting the portrait, asked Fletcher for more details. The manservant revealed the staff members' intense dislike for the painting and bowed courteously before making his way down the corridor and out of sight.

Before closing his bedroom door, Lieutenant Hodgeson took another close look at the portrait and, as he prepared for bed, his thoughts turned to Fletcher's comment that the 'Tartan Lady' was said to make an appearance on the

The southern front of Blackwell Grange.

anniversary of the Battle of Culloden which took place on 16 April 1746. The very next day would mark the seventy-fifth anniversary of that battle, in which his own regiment had taken part, and Hodgeson pondered this coincidence while he drifted off to sleep.

At around 2 a.m. he woke suddenly and immediately became aware of a bright white light on the central section of the bedroom door. Sitting bolt upright, he gazed in amazement as the light spread to assume a human shape, which passed through the door and moved towards him. As the brightness faded he could clearly make out a tall lady dressed in white with a red tartan sash draped from her shoulder but, as fear gripped him, Robert Hodgeson found that he was unable to move.

With her arms outstretched the female apparition moved towards him with eyes and face full of menace. At last the soldier stirred from his trance, seized his pistols and fired first at the head and then at the chest of the ghostly female. Slowly the spectre sank lower and lower and then shrunk into a tiny round light that moved across the floor until it reached the door and faded away through the panels.

The silence was broken by a loud hammering on the door and, as Hodgeson edged it open, he was met by the manservant Fletcher with a lamp in his hand and a worried look on his face. As he recovered his composure the soldier explained, in halting tones, about his encounter with the spectre of the Tartan Lady. The pair turned to look down the corridor to where the portrait of the Tartan Lady hung.

Slowly approaching the painting, the two men could make out a hazy green mist around the portrait and they halted abruptly. Hodgeson then pointed excitedly towards the figure and picked out the burned mark of a bullet hole on her forehead. Closer inspection showed another hole in the white dress where the woman's heart would have been located.

In later correspondence to his cousin, George Allan, Robert Hodgeson explained the sequence of events during his stay at Blackwell Grange but Allan refused to hear of any supernatural influences in the episode. He was quite sure that Hodgeson's frightening experiences were related to some sort of nightmare but, nevertheless, he gave Fletcher instructions to destroy the damaged portrait. According to reports, many members of the household staff were pleased and relieved to see the end of the portrait.

Since then, though some people claim that the 'Tartan Lady' has been seen around the house and grounds, quieter times have prevailed at Blackwell Grange. A later member of the family, Robert, married Hannah Havelock and the family became Havelock-Allan. Sir Henry Havelock-Allan had a distinguished military career that culminated in his decoration with the Victoria Cross by Queen Victoria on 8 June 1859. He died from wounds sustained in an attack by Afridi warriors in the Khyber Pass on 30 December 1897.

This impressive building's status as a major hotel venue was confirmed on 19 September 1972 when it was announced that a peace conference was to be held within its walls. The intention was to find a possible solution to the 'Troubles' in Northern Ireland with deliberations led by the Ulster Secretary at the time, Willie Whitelaw, in conjunction with Brian Faulkner representing the Unionist Party.

The Foresters Arms

Down the centuries, until the completion of a modern road system, Coatham Mundeville was a thriving community beside the Great North Road. There are traces of those earlier periods of occupation in nearby open countryside and echoes of earlier times at the Foresters Arms, which hosts a whole range of community-based activities and events, including a Ukulele Club and Reptile Society.

Perhaps it is ghostly presences from previous centuries that are linked to a series of non-threatening incidents at this vibrant roadside inn. These include items being inexplicably moved around, pumps at the bar mysteriously turning on and the landlady being locked in the cellar overnight after the door had closed behind her.

The Foresters Arms, Coatham Mundeville.

Hall Garth Hotel and Country Club

The Hall Garth Hotel and Country Club is set in some 70 acres of parkland, about 4 miles to the north of Darlington town centre, and has all the features of a stylish modern hotel. However, some of the older parts of its fabric are linked with a tantalising supernatural tale.

Parts of the range of buildings date from the sixteenth, seventeenth and eighteenth centuries, with a nearby deer house adding a contrast in styles with its early nineteenth-century features. Most of the spectral incidents focus on room 2, where guests have reported unexplained happenings such as bathroom taps turning themselves on at the same time during the night time, and investigators link such events with earlier days when monks were based on the site.

It seems that an unfortunate nun was immured (buried alive) between two walls after it was discovered that she was having an affair with one of the resident monks.

Hall Garth Country Hotel.

Redworth Hall

Located about 8 miles north of Darlington and set within 150 acres of woodlands, Redworth Hall is a popular four-star hotel, spa and wedding venue. The nearby village was first mentioned in documents dating from 1183 and during the medieval period the old manor house and estate of Redworth were owned by the Crosier family.

Parts of the existing building date from 1693 but after assuming ownership in 1744, Lord Robert Surtees carried out extensive rebuilding work. He created an impressive two-storeyed sandstone mansion with gabled attics that include many original features such as a superb galleried Baronial Great Hall and an ornate spiral stone staircase. Robert Surtees' nephew and heir, also Robert Surtees, extended the hall in 1820 and the family continued to live at Redworth until the death, in 1955, of Henry Surtees. For a number of years it was used as a residential school before undergoing adaptations as a hotel.

During this latest phase of the building's history, Redworth Hall has had numerous reports of supernatural activity that, for the most part, are linked to two different ghosts ... a child and a scullery maid.

It is widely believed that Lord Robert Surtees had a mentally ill child who he used to keep chained to a fireplace in the hall. This cruel treatment, so it is claimed, accounts for the sightings of a small child seen wondering along the corridors of the hotel. On other occasions, residents have reported being wakened during the night by a child's screams and a child has reportedly been spotted through the viewfinder of many of the digital cameras positioned in the hall.

Other reported sightings are linked to a female apparition who has been observed walking the corridors of the hall looking for her lost love. It is believed that this supernatural presence is a scullery maid who became pregnant with Lord Surtees' child during an illicit affair. When Lady Surtees discovered the truth, speculation

Redworth Hall.

suggests that the maid committed suicide by throwing herself down the stairs.

At other times, guests have complained about feeling as if someone or something was jumping on the bed, while others have reported a sensation of being watched and occasions where electrical appliances have switched on and off by themselves. Most of these incidents were linked to rooms 7 and 14 within Redworth Hall.

While the vast majority of Redworth's ghostly visitations remain tantalisingly unexplained, one night-time episode during 2005 had a humorous outcome. The Bangladeshi cricket team were staying at the hotel during their summer tour of England and, after hearing of the building's supernatural activity, it is perhaps easy to imagine their response when they heard the sound of a child crying during the hours of darkness.

The touring team's captain, Habibul Bashar, showed commendable courage and leadership qualities by rushing into the corridor to confront the ghostly menace. During the ensuing commotion several other hotel guests were woken and their displeasure was compounded when the apparition proved to be none other than the Bangladeshi's fast bowler and practical joker Mashrafe Mortaza who was carrying a bed sheet and a tape recorder.

THREE

SPOOKY RESIDENTIAL AREAS

THE HAREWOOD HILL area on the west side of Darlington is often described as the most haunted area of the town. In its early days the district was called the Glassensikes with 'glassene' meaning blue or grey and 'sike' representing an old legal term for a minor watercourse.

One of the many ghostly tales linked with this area is set on an eerie moonlit night when a local gentleman was returning at about midnight from an outing to Oxen-le-Field. As he approached Harewood Hill the lone walker was astonished to see the head of a large animal appear from behind a stile. The dark black head was followed by an equally dark body of unprecedented size and a similarly outsized tail. With a bound the giant dog leapt to the centre of the road before positioning itself to stare at the man.

The Glassensikes hound stood perfectly still with a fixed stare directed towards the traveller. Try as he might, waving his arms and trying to shoo the dog away, the walker was unable to get it to budge. Until this moment he had been totally of the opinion that the Glassensikes hound was a figment of other folks' imagination but now, as fear and panic took hold, he turned on his heel and began a headlong dash to safer ground.

Some of the phantoms of Harewood Hill have not put in an appearance since housing spread over most of the area and numbered among these is the headless man who disappeared in a ball of fire. His rural residence was said to be located in a boggy field near the Glassensikes (and no doubt cynics pointed out the likely presence of nothing more sinister than methane as a reason for the flaming presence).

Another headless ghost lurked around Prescott's stile on the footpath between Harewood and Blackwell where the Prescott family home was located. This residence, known as the Old Manor House, was said to be haunted by 'Old Pinkney' who paraded the rooms and corridors wearing a red nightcap. A well that served the building – 'Pinkney's Well' – was apparently never used to draw water after nightfall for fear of encountering this colourful spirit.

Among other ghostly revelations that were divulged at a lecture given in 1888 were the antics of another phantom in Harewood Grove whose presence was revealed by the sound of rustling silk garments. By way of amusement this strange presence resorted to breaking spiritual sticks (incense sticks used in times past to enhance magical powers) or hauling chairs across the floor, and its appearances were even weirder. Emerging from beneath a bed, it displayed only half of a human male head before clambering into the bed and taking on the form of a child. On occasions, it used clay cold hands to lift itself halfway out of its resting place.

Such tales were undoubtedly met with a considerable measure of disbelief and ridicule when first related, and in many instances they were probably referred to as the fanciful fabrications of a disturbed mind. However, others gave them credence and one nineteenth-century historian wrote, '… It is true that these awful visions occasionally resolved themselves into a pony shackled in an adjoining field, or Stamper's white dog, or a pair of sweethearts under the cold moon, but still a vast amount of credible evidence exists about the fallen glories of the night-roaming ghost of Glassensikes.'

Quite why the Harewood Hill area of Darlington should attract so many haunted episodes is not at all clear. Could it be to do with the lie of the land or earlier dramatic episodes, perhaps the type of properties scattered around the district or even the state of mind of local folk? Belief in witchcraft and the power of the devil persisted in some places until quite recent times and it seems that in their hour of need some residents turned to well-respected figures for help and guidance.

Reports suggest that during the early nineteenth century one local woman, in a distressed state, visited Mr Edward Pease and explained that she could not work because a ghost was inclined to sit on the head of her spinning wheel. Because of these interruptions, which meant that she could not complete her tasks, she was in danger of starving. The woman was quite sure that Mr Pease could remove the ghost and implored him to do so. He agreed to help the unfortunate woman and took a piece of paper which he then decorated with some large 'B's and red wafers. After holding it close to the fire, Mr Pease then attached it to the wheel head. Not long afterwards the grateful woman joyfully informed her benefactor that the persistent ghost had now vanished.

A large proportion of ghostly sightings take place during the hours of darkness but there were daytime visitations in the Darlington area too. Reports in the *Northern Despatch and Echo* on 26 April 1938 describe a white headless figure, seen in broad daylight, emerging out of the door of an embattled cow house behind Polam. The spectre is said to have walked at a leisurely pace around the building before vanishing at the corner. Local folk came to the conclusion that the spooky figure was most likely the spirit of a man who had hanged himself in the building and was then unable to rest in his grave.

Down the years Blackwell Lane has gained quite a reputation as the setting for sudden death and hauntings. Perhaps the best-known episode was linked to the sad demise of Cicely Kirby, a young servant girl in the neighbourhood.

Details of the mysterious hauntings were explained in a book by Dr Manson, who retold events in 1745 surrounding the rebellion led by Bonnie Prince Charlie. As they moved northwards the king's troops were billeted in Darlington and it was then that a soldier, Sam Addy, ended the life of young Cicely.

His ghastly secret remained concealed until after the Battle of Culloden when Addy lay seriously wounded on the battlefield. As fate would have it, Sam Addy and Cicely's lover, Jack Langstaffe, lay wounded side by side when 'a greenish light began to suffuse itself into the tent and both saw standing before them Cicely Kirby. For a few seconds it stood there and then, raising its hands as in entreaty, slowly disappeared from sight without appearing to move from the spot where it stood …'

Through his grief Jack Langstaffe explained the depth of his feelings for Cicely and, as dawn broke and his final moments neared, Addy confessed how he had met the unfortunate servant girl on Blackwell Lane. Consumed with jealousy for her other suitors, he accosted her but as she fought back, and then stumbled, fell and struck her head against a tree root. As she lay motionless Addy thought at first that she was already dead but then, realising that she was still breathing, he determined to end her life.

He admitted to Langstaffe that he had strangled her with his handkerchief and had then hidden her body under bushes. Soon afterwards Sam Addy and Jack Langstaffe breathed their last on the battlefield.

More than a century after the brutal killing, in 1853, workmen removing a hedge in Blackwell Lane uncovered the skeleton of a young woman. Her body had been buried doubled up and, as well as her teeth being in almost perfect condition, parts of her clothes and shoes were still attached to her mortal remains. As far as is known, the workmen reburied her body at the same spot.

During the early 1900s, stories circulated in the Blackwell area that a simple roadside stone marked the spot where a soldier had murdered his lover. Rumours persisted that animals had repeatedly scratched the surface in that area and whenever the pathway was repaired a hole was always there again by the following morning.

In 1935 a road worker named Walter Wake was excavating a wider roadway when he uncovered traces of the earlier, ancient route and what appeared to be a turnip. Closer inspection established that it was in fact a human bone and further careful clearance of the soil exposed a whole skeleton.

Again the remains of Cicely Kirby were carefully reinterred and hopefully her spirit was laid to rest for all time.

More Fearsome Phantoms

Perhaps it was because of the number of open areas of ground with no streetlights to help explain and identify uncanny noises and shapes among clumps of woodland that Darlington had local residents who went in fear of such an assortment of ghosts.

If Harewood Hill and Blackwell laid claim to being the most haunted locations then close behind, in ghostly terms, must have been land between Stanhope Road and Bondgate (now dissected by Abbey Road). The *North Star* of 3 April 1907 reported how these meadows were regarded as being dark and 'fearsome' by more cautious residents. One particular location adding to this sense of foreboding was a plantation with a small central clearing in the middle of which stood Laurel Cottage.

The newspaper report explained that about fifty years earlier (in the late 1850s) a teetotal businessman and his wife were returning to their home at about midnight and had reached the location now known as Stanhope Green. At this point the gentleman, perhaps aware of a nearby presence, looked round and caught sight of an old woman in a long trailing dress coming towards him. His surprise turned to amazement when the female figure melted through the dense hedge (rather than climb it or find a way to bypass it) before disappearing into the field beyond.

There were further sightings of the unknown apparition when the couple returned from visiting friends in Greenbank Road but on each occasion the businessman's wife remained blissfully unaware of his observations. He, meanwhile, did not wish to alarm his spouse, but then one evening events took a dramatic turn when one of their maidservants also saw the ghost.

On the evening in question, their maidservant suddenly rushed into the house in a most distressed state of mind and promptly fainted. When she recovered her senses sufficiently, the maid was able to explain that she was out walking with a suitor when a ghostly woman appeared from the Greenbank area and began crossing the fields towards them. As news of the sighting spread the story gathered pace as other local folk added their experiences of similar supernatural incidents.

An aunt of the maid recalled similar occurrences in the neighbourhood when she was a child and a local preacher spoke about events in the locality some twenty years before. He remembered open ground at the top of Bondgate, opposite West Lodge, where a small dwelling, Laurel Cottage, stood just a few yards from the roadside. The churchman was also a class leader in the Methodist Church and, whilst staying at Laurel Cottage, had gone to his bedroom, before a service, to commune with God. On a number of occasions he felt as if there was another presence in his room, there was the sound of crumpling newspaper and on one occasion someone came from behind and covered him with a shroud. The strange incidents reached such a pitch that he stopped going into the room.

Then, when his niece arrived from the Halifax area, she stayed overnight in the room only to be almost frightened to death when an old woman wearing a long 'coal-scuttle' bonnet appeared from behind the window curtains and made her way across the room towards the bed. According to the niece, the ghostly female had put her face almost touching her own before vanishing out of sight. Needless to say, she swiftly moved to another room.

A few weeks later the churchman's sister also slept overnight in the haunted room but left early the next morning after just the single night of what should have been a week-long stay. Some years later, when the preacher had moved to another house in Darlington, his sister explained her reasons for the rapid departure. It seems that she had experienced the same unnerving attention from a ghostly woman as the niece but had remained silent about the matter in order to avoid upsetting her brother's wife.

Reports about the supernatural episodes drew letters in the *Darlington and Stockton Times* and conclusions were reached about Laurel Cottage's mysterious background. It seems that the property had a reputation as a house of ill fame and its notoriety spread still further when a wealthy pedlar, who regularly stayed there while on business in the neighbourhood, was murdered by the old woman who owned the cottage.

Local gossip suggested that when she later died, her spirit was not allowed to rest and it haunted the cottage and nearby plantation. When Laurel Cottage was demolished to make way for housing on Granville Terrace, which later became part of Woodland Road, the builder John Hindle uncovered a pile of earth and stones. Further investigation unearthed a male skeleton and the assumption was that it must be the earthly remains of the murdered pedlar.

Again, cynics explained the sequence of supernatural sightings as no more than clouds of marsh gas that spread from nearby ponds and marshland.

Assorted Wraiths on a Busy Road

The busy route that linked Cockerton to central Darlington gained a reputation from early times as a haunted thoroughfare. Much of this fear probably dated from 1242 when an innocent traveller by the name of Thomas Broadhead was murdered by a vagrant called Allan Halkerbain. Discovery of the body was made by the local pinder (the villager responsible for impounding cattle) and tales of Broadhead's reappearance persisted for many years. Roadside trees and vegetation offered hiding places for robbers and other criminals and their furtive, fleeting

Cockerton village green in the late nineteenth century.

Cockerton Bridge in the late nineteenth century.

movements probably only added to the fear among local travellers. Smugglers at coastal and inland locations often fabricated frightening tales – again involving phantoms – in an attempt to deter closer investigation of their nefarious activities.

Many years after the murder of Thomas Broadhead another tragic episode added to fears of unpleasant visions on this route. A young soldier had grown increasingly tired of the strains and stresses of military life and hanged himself from a tree close to the site of Holy Trinity church. The soldier's ghost added to eerie spectres and unnerving sounds that were encountered in the area.

During the second half of the nineteenth century, gas works were constructed in many provincial towns and when 'Cockerton Lane' (as this route was known) was due to have a gas main installed in the 1860s, local residents organised a huge petition demanding that the maximum number of gas lamps should be installed. At last, it seems, there would be no more shadows to hide in.

Unnerving Incidents at Mowden Hall

Several of Darlington's fine Victorian buildings, including the market hall and old town hall along with Barclays Bank on the High Row, were the work of locally based architect Alfred Waterhouse. His impressive design features are also on display at Mowden Hall, towards the town's western perimeter, which was built at a cost of £13,195 as the home of Edwin Lucas Pease.

When Edwin Pease died in 1889 as a result of a hunting accident, the estate passed to his eldest son, William, who played a major role in local business and political circles as chairman of the Cleveland Bridge Engineering Company, director of Consett Ironworks and Conservative MP for Darlington in 1923. Reports indicate that between 8,000 and 10,000 people attended his funeral in 1926.

The last member of the Pease family to live at Mowden Hall was William's brother, Captain Ernest Hubert Pease,

A modern view of Mowden Hall, on the western outskirts of Darlington.

and when he moved south due to ill health in 1927 the hall was leased to Mostyn Hustler. Within months he disposed of the buildings' contents in a three-day sale and then auctioned the hall during 1930.

For a while Mowden Hall was used as a boys' preparatory school and during the Second World War it was occupied by RAF and army personnel. In 1953 this fine building served as the head office of Summerson's Foundries and after several further changes of ownership it was eventually acquired by the Ministry of Public Buildings and Works (now the Department for the Environment) in March 1966 at a cost of £30,000.

Many of the building's original features, including elaborate wooden panelling, are still in place and regular reports suggest that rooms, corridors and staircases are frequented by supernatural forces.

Members of staff have often told of incidents where doors were banged shut and locked by an unseen presence, while cleaners, security personnel, administration support staff and outside contractors have all been unnerved by a feeling that an eerie presence was watching them at work. One cleaner said that she felt someone pass her in the corridor as she was vacuuming, without hearing a door open or close, and a joiner working at the rear of the premises always felt the hair on the back of his neck rise whenever he entered the servants' quarters.

One member of staff actually reported the presence of a 'grey lady' standing beside her on the staircase close to her workplace and further credence was given to the catalogue of spectral incidents by workmen who experienced a number of inexplicable events while they were based at the hall in the late 1990s.

Health and safety regulations required that renovation work was completed outside normal office hours and the workmen recalled that the ghostly incidents invariably began soon after midnight. Doors banged shut and then opened again after they had been locked, and on one occasion a flying cork travelled across the room and landed at the feet of the bemused workmen. Once, after they had left in the early hours of the morning, a security guard checked the area where they had been working and found all the lights switched on even though the incredulous workmen were adamant that they had turned everything off before leaving.

So far the identity of the 'grey lady' and possible reasons for the series of mysterious incidents remain unexplained.

FOUR

HAUNTED TOWN CENTRE LOCATIONS

As with most town and city centres up and down the country, Darlington has seen any amount of closures, demolition and redevelopment but in the midst of this fast-moving, ever-changing world who can say that the supernatural presences reported in central locations no longer exist?

Arguably Darlington's most famous ghost is Lady Jarrett – or Gerrard – whose sad demise is linked with violent times during the English Civil War. The setting for this shocking episode was the Bishop of Durham's manor house, which stood on ground between St Cuthbert's church and the modern town hall buildings.

After marrying Sir Gilbert Gerrard, Constable of Billingham, Lady Jarrett, a daughter of Dr John Cosin, Bishop of Durham, was resident at the manor house when marauding Parliamentarian troops burst into the premises. Their demands for money were vehemently rejected but an expensive ring on her finger soon caught the soldiers' attention. One of the troops covered her mouth to stifle any pleas for help while another soldier seized Lady Jarrett's hand, but all attempts to remove the ring by force were disappointed as it remained firmly in place.

Undeterred, one of the soldiers drew his sword and savagely hacked off Lady Jarrett's left arm. As the two attackers made off with their prize her ladyship staggered towards the wall before slumping lifeless to the floor. Tradition claims that her bloodstained right hand left a clear crimson mark down the wall as she fell. Despite numerous attempts to remove the distinctive mark it remained, clear for all to see, on the wall of the manor house.

From that time there were reports of the ghost of Lady Jarrett walking through the room where she was murdered or of her sitting on the boundary wall of the nearby churchyard. The female apparition was easily identified as she had only one arm and, as the number of sightings increased, Lady Jarrett's spirit is said to have made a nightly trek along a subterranean passage from the manor house to St Cuthbert's church.

A late nineteenth-century view of Darlington Market with the Boot and Shoe Hotel in the background.

In due course the bishop's manor house was adapted as the town's workhouse but the ghostly visitations continued. At times, in a playful mood, she is said to have banged pans, rattled an old pump handle and pulled bedclothes off servants' beds, but Lady Jarrett's actions were usually aimed at showing kindness towards occupants of the workhouse. Helpful gestures such as making coffee for the sick earned her the unofficial title of 'Lady Charity' but the only indication of her presence was the rustling of her white silk dress.

Reported sightings added to the mystic aura surrounding Lady Jarrett and at least one of these had an unfortunate outcome. A small-time pedlar with basic premises in the down-town Leadyard rented a market stall each Monday but, with limited stock, he had to transfer stock from shop to stall using a group of local lads to transport items. Late one Monday evening, after a long day of labouring at the market, the boys were moving unsold items back to the Leadyard shop when a pale face appeared from behind a wall. It seemed to be on the point of speaking when one of the youths blurted out '… Lady Jarrett, Lady Jarrett!'. Without hesitation the group of lads dropped the goods they were carrying, turned and ran, leaving an array of broken items in the gutter.

During 1870 the former bishop's manor house was sold to Richard Luck for £2,000 and in later correspondence he described the events that occurred as demolition work got underway …

49

The end room was where Lady Jarrett was murdered and the bloodstains which could not be washed off were there. I was soon very much engaged in my work when I heard footsteps coming out of this room and I could feel it was her Ladyship. I could hear the rustle of her silk dress and she came close until I could feel her breath and her dress as she stooped over my shoulder to see what I was doing. I stood it for a very short while and then bolted along the corridor as hard as I could go.

All traces of the bishop's manor house were removed by Darlington Corporation workmen in 1938 and there have been no more reported sightings since then. However, it is said, perhaps mischievously, that the swirl of silk garments has been heard along the corridors of Darlington town hall …

Perhaps it is of little surprise that so many hostelries – pubs, inns, hotels and the like – are haunted. Many of the buildings have been around for centuries and within their walls there have been all sorts of events and occasions, ranging from joyous celebrations to riotous and violent confrontations culminating in murder and mayhem.

The Boot and Shoe Hotel on Church Row may well trace its name back to a time when Darlington was a centre for tanning and leather making businesses. The upper floors of this distinctive building are said to be haunted by a domestic girl who died in the attic many years ago, while one of the bars is also the setting for sightings of a stout male figure wearing a leather apron. Speculation among staff and customers suggests that he may well have been a local blacksmith.

The Boot and Shoe Hotel.

A Helpful Soul

The King's Head Hotel on Priestgate featured prominently as a coaching inn and may date – at least in part – from 1611. Indeed, it is claimed that parish council meetings were held on the premises during the eighteenth century with refreshment provided from the rates! The last couple of centuries have seen extensive programmes of refurbishment but one long-term resident is said to be a friendly spirit known as Albert the Butler. He has been around for over 100 years and his activities usually take place on the fourth floor. Albert's generous gestures include helping guests with their packing and unpacking and even extend, if reports are to be believed, to leaving a nightcap of whisky in guests' rooms even though it had not been requested.

Other guests have reported ghostly sightings of a young girl dressed in Victorian clothing, including a bonnet and bow tied under her chin.

Junction of High Row in 1930.

The King's Head Hotel in the late nineteenth century.

51

Haunting of an Iconic Building

Darlington's Covered Market was constructed on a central site in the town after the Local Government Board went ahead with plans during the early 1860s for a new and more hygienic venue for displaying foodstuffs. Initial opposition to the scheme was soon overcome and total building costs amounted to £16,356 8s 9d.

Designs for the scheme, which included the town hall and town clock, were prepared by Alfred Waterhouse, who became this country's foremost Victorian Gothic-style architect, and the Covered Market soon became a focal point for everyday life in Darlington. Surprisingly perhaps, there was no official opening ceremony and this may well have resulted from a tragic incident at the site in December 1863. The Tenth Annual Show of the Northern Counties Fat Cattle and Poultry Society was held at the premises while building work was still in progress and, during proceedings, collapsing masonry resulted in one man sustaining fatal injuries. The first public event at the completed Covered Market took place in early December 1864 with the Eleventh Annual Show of the same society.

Cellars beneath the building provided storage space, fire engine rooms, plumbers' shops and lamp rooms. It was this area that featured in reports of ghostly activity, often at dead of night, and mostly witnessed by the market foreman, Frank Hutchinson. Now retired after twenty-three years service in the post, he recalled being regularly called out in the 1980s and 1990s and always, it seems, in the early hours after the market's alarms had inexplicably rung down in the basement of the building.

The clock tower of Darlington market hall in 1930.

A modern view of the clock tower.

High Row, Darlington, in the late nineteenth century.

Market day at Darlington in the late nineteenth century.

54

On a number of occasions Frank caught sight of a female phantom. Dressed all in white, she emerged from under the wooden door of the old town hall and continued directly ahead through a solid brick wall. Speculation about her identity has provided any number of possible explanations with some suggesting a link to Darlington's first police cell, which was on the site of the Covered Market. Perhaps she was arrested, detained there, and with time to reflect on the enormity of her crime, she committed suicide. Other theories feature more gruesome conclusions by highlighting the fact that she walks across the site of the old shambles (meat market) where she may have been constantly attempting to leave her butcher boyfriend. Just possibly, so the speculation runs, he took up his cleaver and dealt her a fatal blow.

However, a joyful atmosphere prevailed on 7 and 8 June 2013 when the Darlington Covered Market celebrated 150 years of operations. Events included the town's first public ox roast since 1902, a Victorian-style workshop, swing boats, treasure hunts and live music.

When is a Ghost not a Ghost?

Years ago rumours abounded that a property in Tubwell Row was haunted by an apparition that became known as the 'Coffee-ghost'. Residents became unnerved by the activities of the spectre – which some folk claimed was the ghost of a former apprentice – which kept grinding away at a coffee mill. Eventually, one brave soul ventured closer to the irritating sounds and found – no doubt to everyone's great relief – that the creaking and grinding sounds were caused by ... an ill-fitting door. Leaving the door only slightly open rendered it silent!

Tubwell Row in 1907.

A late nineteenth-century view of Tubwell Row – a busy scene with trains and carriages.

Quieter times on Tubwell Row – looking east in 1920.

Properties on Tubwell Row in 1959.

Tubwell Row photographed in 2014.

Darlington Memorial Hospital's 'Grey Lady'

Darlington's growth as an industrial and commercial centre during the second half of the nineteenth century brought the need for improved medical facilities and in 1865 the town's first public hospital and dispensary opened in Russell Street. Some twenty years later the grey brick New Hospital buildings were completed on a site in Greenbank Road to designs by George Gordon Hoskins. Additional construction work was later carried out but, during the interwar years, the town's main focus of medical care shifted to a site on Hollyhurst Road where Darlington Memorial Hospital was officially opened on Friday, 5 May 1933 by HRH Prince George, KG, GCVO.

Expansion of facilities and redevelopment of the site in recent years left the 'Memorial Hall' as the only remaining part of the original hospital with most of the older building sited on what became the visitors' car park.

Shortly after his retirement, a former engineer at the Memorial Hospital recalled an unnerving incident at the site during 2010. On the day in question, he was asked to investigate reports of a possible steam leak in a tunnel below the buildings. Essential services such as gas and water ran through the tunnel, which was composed of two sections. One of these, he explained, was used to transfer bodies down to the mortuary lift and to allow access for engineering staff during bad weather, while the other section, into which he had never previously ventured, carried the essential services.

Darlington Memorial Hospital.

Approaching the entrance to the tunnel along an uphill gradient, he could hear the sound of leaking steam just beyond a white-painted wooden door. Easing his way through the tunnel door, which he then closed gently behind him, the engineer began to carry out repairs on the leak, only for his concentration to be seriously disturbed by the sound of a door opening. A glance over his shoulder showed the white door slowly opening and, as he watched, the full length of the tunnel came into view to show the uphill section that he had followed. The door stood open for what seemed like several minutes before slamming shut again.

Alone in the tunnel, the engineer's mind began to race. One immediate conclusion was that there was an unseen person behind the door so he ran down and opened it fully against the back wall. No one could possibly hide behind it and the bare walls of the tunnel offered no other hiding places … feeling increasingly ill at ease, he requested assistance so that he wouldn't have to continue working alone in the tunnel. Nothing was mentioned to his fellow workman at the time but a couple of months later the engineer described the episode to another colleague whose immediate reply was … 'Oh so you have met the Grey Lady!'

Unexpected Responses in 'Remedies'

Reports in the *Northern Echo* during September 1996 highlighted a series of strange incidents in a shop named 'Remedies' in Clark's Yard off High Row. The first occurred in April 1995 when a cat statue fell from a shelf where it had been safely positioned and was found in pieces under the till counter. Staff members found it extremely strange that the statue should have fallen in the first place and then have travelled so far across the shop floor to its final resting place.

On another occasion, all the shop lights were switched on after staff had left the building in complete darkness. Shortly afterwards, this episode was being retold to a sales representative when a shop light went out and the startled business visitor left the premises rather quickly.

Clark's Yard (off High Row).

Office equipment in the shop also mysteriously disappeared before reappearing unexpectedly – for instance, a tagging system vanished for a while and then turned up without reason in a jewellery box!

The shop owner was a spiritual healer and decided to try and make direct contact with the ghostly presence. The name Jemima Thomkinson came to her and it appeared that Jemima may have died when a horse fell on her, with further research revealing that a stable once stood on the site of the shop.

A Vow of Spectral Silence

During the post-war years, vehicles of the United Bus Company were a familiar sight on north-east roads. Based originally in Lowestoft, Suffolk, under the leadership of E.B. Hutchinson, operations expanded rapidly throughout Norfolk, Suffolk and Lincolnshire and in the autumn of 1912 the first north-east depot was opened at Bishop Auckland.

Further phases of expansion followed during the 1920s and in 1932 the headquarters of the company moved to Grange Road, Darlington, where a new engineering works was built on the same site. In the 1950s new employees were told about a ghostly presence on the premises but also sworn to secrecy about the spectre.

It transpires that the rear of the premises stood on part of an ancient dwelling or convent and the cellar was used by United for storing documents. At the end of each financial year all out-of-date documents were gathered in the fireplace for the caretaker to burn but nobody would enter the cellar alone, even when all of the lights were switched on.

A possible explanation for this state of affairs was provided by a long-serving member of staff in conversation with a new employee. It was explained that, '... When the house was a large home of a monied man, a maid employed by the family was made pregnant by the owner of the house. The child was born and seemed totally normal apart from a birthmark which seemed to prove, beyond doubt, that the master of the house was its father ...' With such a clear indication of its parentage, the child's father took matters to a dramatic and sinister conclusion. At dead of night he removed the newborn baby from its cot and took it to the cellar where he burnt it in the fireplace. According to reports, on the following morning, the distraught mother ended her own life.

Since those days, reports persisted of a young woman in servant's clothes who was seen walking along the corridor, wringing her hands as she stumbled along, as if she was searching for something. Any number of explanations could be drawn from her movements, but crucially she always ended her supernatural travels at the fireplace ...

Later decades of the twentieth century saw endless changes to coach services, including deregulation of local bus operations in 1986. During 1994 a new head office and engineering works was built in Morton Road, Darlington, as a replacement for the town's Grange Road premises. Two years later the Cowie Group – now named Arriva – took over United and other bus companies in a £280 million buyout of the British Bus Group that made it one of the country's top three bus operators.

Unscheduled Theatrical Appearances

It is hardly surprising that so many theatres up and down the country boast at least one resident ghost. With such a range of performances, from light-hearted comedies to historical masterpieces and doleful tragedies, there can be little wonder that phantoms of all descriptions prowl the stage, stalls and other parts of theatrical venues.

Darlington Civic Theatre first opened its doors as the New Hippodrome and Palace of Varieties on Monday, 2 September 1907 under its founder and first managing director, Signor Rino Pepi. An Italian by upbringing, he had abandoned academic studies as a young student to develop a theatrical career as a quick-change artist and impersonator. His act included a fifteen-minute sketch entitled *Love Always Victorious* in which he played all seven parts – both male and female – and he could also sing tenor and soprano.

During 1895, at the age of 34, Rino Pepi moved to London and topped the bill at the London Pavilion for three months. He had already toured Austria, Belgium and Holland with an appearance before Queen Victoria and, as his career in England developed, Baron Rothschild became a strong admirer. Supported by Cinquevalli – the only juggler ever to balance three billiard balls on the end of a cue – Pepi performed at the banker's London mansion.

He was at the height of his career, aged 35, when he suddenly gave up performing and set out on a new venture in management with his first project in the north-east. Initially Rino Pepi succeeded – in part because he was an extremely popular personality, highly regarded for his charm and culture as well as his generosity – but as the film industry prospered so theatres suffered a decline in popularity.

Signor Pepi died in November 1927 at the age of 66, on the same day as the ballet legend, Pavlova, performed her 'Dying Swan' in the fading spotlight at Darlington's Hippodrome Theatre. He was buried in full dress suit alongside his wife, Italian Countess Rosette, at Barrow in Furness, but regular supernatural sightings suggest that he is still around – in spirit at least – keeping an eye on theatre operations.

Down the years there has been a whole catalogue of incidents, with many of them linking to Rino Pepi.

Darlington Civic Theatre.

Staff members heard footsteps in empty corridors, doors shut on their own and usherettes were tapped on their shoulders only to find no one behind them. There were also sightings of a Pekinese dog and some people believed it to be the ghost of Signor Pepi's pet canine. On one occasion, a small boy visiting the theatre's coffee bar suddenly jumped up, spilling his drink. He blamed his sudden action on the appearance of a small black dog and, when told that there was no dog in the theatre, he described it as having '… a squashed face and goggly eyes'.

An intriguing twist to this particular spooky tale came with the discovery of skeletal remains, in a wall, of what was believed to be Signor Pepi's Pekinese, during refurbishment of the theatre in 1990.

Reports continued when the stage manager heard a party going on in room 11 late one night, but when he went to check there was no one there. An actress and a member of the audience saw an unknown woman on the stage during a production but had no idea who it was. Actors using dressing room 12 reported a baby crying but there was no sign inside or outside of an infant, while, on another occasion, an actress returned to the room after searching the landing outside for a crying child only to see a baby looking back at her in the mirror. Unsurprisingly the actress promptly asked for a different dressing room! Most incidents, though, had a link to Rino Pepi. Cleaners reported that seat HH13 in the dress circle must have been his usual place because when they went about their work in the mornings his was the only seat down, as though he had sat there during the previous evening or night.

Such a wealth of supernatural spectres has perhaps inevitably led to investigations at the theatre by ghost-hunting groups in recent years. A visit by Paranormal Companies reported that members of the team were sitting in the middle stalls with the rear door leading to the bar area partially open to afford a limited view when they heard a sound that could only be described as a door being kicked. The group immediately jumped up and made a thorough search of the area where they were sitting and of the adjacent bar area but there was no sign of a human presence. No one was heard running away from the immediate area or adjacent rooms.

During the same visit the whole group of investigators were sitting on the stage when a number of them, who were looking in the same direction, saw a flash of light from the opposite side of the middle stalls … as though someone had been in this higher section to turn a light on for a brief moment. Again no one was there, no door was seen to have opened to allow people to leave the area and nor was anyone heard running away. Further research by members of the group indicated that the building was also haunted by a flyman (who worked the ropes that moved scenery around and were often former sailors with experience of rigging) and a nightwatchman.

In the early days of April 2004 a group of Yorkshire Psychic Investigators carried out a study at Darlington Civic Theatre (as the former Hippodrome is now known) using sound and image recording equipment. They highlighted significant activity in the dress circle, on the fly floor and in dressing room 12, while a medium noted a ghostly presence backstage – with an Italian connection and the initials 'S.R.P.' Digital imaging also picked up orbs, which are images detecting spirits in the form of a round ball of bright light. The duty manager at the time of the investigations commented on the psychic links with Signor Pepi with the statement: '… We think he's just keeping an eye on things. There isn't any malevolence involved.'

During the last decade Darlington Civic Theatre has staged a series of regular events with a supernatural theme and this splendid building has become recognised by experienced ghost hunters as one of the region's scariest locations.

Some of the ghost vigils at the theatre are held to raise funds for St Teresa's Hospice and on most occasions it seems there is plenty of supernatural activity. On one occasion, a woman was so frightened that she had to leave the evening vigil and return home, while another lady reported seeing the reflection of a young girl. Other members of the group heard whistling from the backstage area and noisy clattering around the stage ladders.

During an organised charity event in August 2012 several female guests reported hearing a quiet voice whisper over a walkie-talkie and a child was heard giggling in another area of the theatre. Guests also reported seeing a figure in a seat in the upper circle … only for it to vanish from view … and another woman claimed that she felt a great weight on her shoulders as if someone was pushing her.

During the summer of 2014, Peter Tate, house manager at the theatre for the last twelve years, reflected on the many emotions – laughter, joy and sadness – that have been witnessed during the building's 107-year history and concluded, 'I think the building records it all.'

A new chapter in the theatre's history was heralded with the announcement, on 8 October 2014, that a bid for £5 million from the Heritage Lottery Fund (HLF) had been successful. Extra funding from other sources will enable a total of £8 million to be spent on renovating Darlington Civic Theatre so that it can compete with other north-east venues.

Proposals include restoration of the Grade II listed building, installation of a new bar in the former water tower, improved seating and better disabled access. Other developments include a new education centre and a gallery area, along with improvements to backstage areas that will allow the theatre to accommodate larger touring companies and more sophisticated stage sets.

Detailed proposals will be considered during the second stage and if these have progressed to the HLF's satisfaction, and are in line with the original proposals, then funding is confirmed.

Work on the project is anticipated to begin during summer 2016 and one is left wondering just how many supernatural sightings there will be during this fascinating phase in the theatre's history.

Unscheduled Sightings of a Supernatural Nature

In May 2011 a series of unexplained, nerve-wracking events were recalled by the former deputy manager of one of Darlington's first theme bars. All the incidents took place after hours and it may be purely coincidental that the building housing the club had previously been used as a holding area for people killed during the war years 1939–45.

On one occasion, after closing time, staff were enjoying a relaxing drink on the lower level when they heard noises from the second floor. They knew that there was no one in the area at that time and the mystery deepened when doors were slammed shut behind members of staff without reason and the music was increased in volume when there was no one in the DJ box.

Events took a more dramatic turn one evening when a few staff members were enjoying an after-hours get-together. The deputy manager was behind the bar sorting out a couple of drinks for colleagues when his attention was caught by a woman in a short flowery dress who was walking up a flight of stairs, probably to visit the toilet. He turned to ask two nearby chaps who she was, but when they looked back she was nowhere in sight. There was no one around but work colleagues and a search of the whole of the second floor failed to locate the mystery female.

On another occasion the deputy manager and a colleague were standing at the end of the bar at about 9.30 p.m. on a wet Tuesday night during winter. There were no customers but the eerie silence was suddenly interrupted by a huge crashing sound from the floor above. Both men were physically shaken by the massive impact but, gathering their wits, they ran upstairs in search of the cause of the crash. As they entered the empty kitchen the contents of a tray of cutlery were scattered all over the floor but the tray itself was still on the worktop … empty.

There were numerous unnerving incidents over a four-year period but none of them could compare to the dramatic end of one particular fairly quiet evening's work. On the day in question the deputy manager was reaching for the under-stairs control box to switch off the lights and activate the security alarm while a colleague began to draw down a large metal shutter over the outer door.

The job was almost done, with all lights apart from the fire route and escape lights extinguished and the metal shutter halfway down, when, for some unknown reason, the deputy manager glanced upwards. At this moment his heart froze for, gazing down from the second-floor balcony, was a monstrous dark shape. Slowly the terrifying apparition took on the appearance of a tall individual wearing the hooded robes of a monk, but it was clearly less than human.

Within a few seconds, with frenzied haste, the deputy manager had tapped the alarm code into the box and sprinted outside with only a brief pause to force the shutter down to ground level. There was no backwards glance towards the huge windows covering the building's frontage as he pulled open his car door and slid into its safe haven.

FIVE

GHOSTLY ANIMALS

IN RECENT centuries a whole range of animals that formerly roamed the great tracts of forest and woodland across northern England have disappeared from the countryside. Wild bears may well have been common until the tenth century AD and creatures such as wolves and boars were hunted until fairly recent times. Then, of course, there is talk in current days of a puma or panther on the loose in parts of Durham or Northumberland and even talk of animals that cannot possibly belong in the realms of the living.

Carving in the wall on Bull Wynd.

The most prevalent North Country malevolence seems to have been the bargest, sometimes referred to as barghest or barguest, which invariably appeared in the form of fiendish dog with large teeth and claws. This fearsome creature was said to have a covering of black fur out of which peered a pair of eyes that had a red (or sometimes yellow) glow. Other attributes of this hellhound were said to be incredible reserves of strength and speed.

Heavily wooded slopes in the Throstlenest area of Darlington were the lair of the town's bargest and people who lived on the south side of Haughton Road would be wakened from their sleep by the horrendous howls of the 'roaring ghost'. Such a clamour was said to be a certain prelude to a tragic event, with one derivation of the name meaning 'carriage for the dead'.

Unwary travellers were likely to be accosted by the bargest, which was said to have the ability to take on different forms – both human and animal – in addition to its usual sighting as a monstrous dog. There was invariably an element of surprise in the bargest's roadside appearances and its stealthy yet speedy movements led to another nickname – 'Padfoot'.

Clearance of woodland for housing and the installation of street lighting brought an end to reported sightings of the bargest in the Throstlenest area but there was an added twist to these tales during the building work itself. A considerable number of human bodies were uncovered at the site, possibly the victims of Scottish raiders or casualties from large-scale encounters such as the Battle of the Standard, or maybe, just maybe, they were killed by the bargest …

Animals and Birds in Phantom Form

Before the advent of motorised transport in the early twentieth century, horses were widely used for travel and, perhaps inevitably, there were also reports of ghostly horses. A phantom brown horse roamed the lanes around Darlington and often blocked the stiles at Harewood and Blackwell, while a white horse was spotted carrying a small child. This was the spirit of a lad aged about 11 whose shining face led to his glowing nickname – 'Radiant Boy'.

A whole range of other animals featured in supernatural reports. Sightings of the ghost of a lamb, particularly in a churchyard, were regarded as most unlucky and the same connotation was applied to swine. This foreboding was taken so seriously that owners of animals found straying into churchyards could be fined. In 1759 Joseph Dixon of Darlington was fined for 'suffering his swine to go at large in the churchyard'.

The appearance of a phantom lamb was taken as an indication that a child was about to die and a sighting of the 'grave sow' – a ghostly pig – was another warning of an imminent death. Linked to these beliefs was the practice of burying such a creature in the foundations of a new building to ensure the long-term safety of the structure.

Phantom cats, meanwhile, were usually linked with ill fortune, probably because of a long-standing belief that witches could change themselves into cats. Traditionally the cat was regarded as the witch's 'familiar'.

In some areas of County Durham ravens were believed to be the souls of murdered men and many village folk

St James' church, Melsonby.

dreaded the overhead calls of the 'gabble ratchets' or Gabriel's Hounds. This distinctive sound was taken as a clear sign that a child in the area was about to die. These 'Gabriel Hounds' were probably bean geese, which emit a strange eerie cry during flight and were believed to be the souls of stillborn or unbaptised children.

The village of Melsonby, near Darlington, has the only recorded mention of a ghost-goose, a pure white bird that was said to haunt Berry Well and nearby churchyard as well as the local neighbourhood.

On one occasion, many years ago, a local farmer was driving his horse and cart along a low lane or roadway leading to Melsonby when his horse suddenly reared up and almost pitched him from his seat before bolting.

As his steed sped along the road the farmer spotted a large white goose waddling solemnly alongside the trap. He was gripped at first with astonishment and then a sense of awe as the goose seemed to be moving slowly but it was keeping pace with the cart. Continuing to watch, the farmer recognised Melsonby churchyard adjacent to the road and at this point the goose passed effortlessly through the closed gate.

On another occasion, two well-known local poachers were returning home with fewer trophies than usual when they spotted a large goose waddling along the roadway in front of them. Silently they crept up behind it and made a firm grab … only to grasp thin air. The goose had vanished without a trace and the pair of poachers are said to have quickly returned home in a state of some bewilderment.

In fact geese were considered to be sacred birds by ancient Britons and often featured in ritual sacrifice. A number of other animal spectres also closely resemble creatures that feature in tales of the Norsemen who invaded and settled in parts of the north-east. Odin's horse, which often journeyed to the underworld, is one such and has reputedly been seen in the area.

In modern times reported sightings of large beasts prowling the countryside are followed up by police forces and Freedom of Information requests have revealed that police authorities in North Yorkshire and County Durham have received more than thirty calls in recent years. An investigator, Mark Fraser of 'Big Cats in Britain', suggested that the figures underestimated reported sightings and that most big cats originated from numerous private zoos in North Yorkshire and the north-east before the Second World War. Their food supply would come from hunting rabbits.

In 2006 a County Durham farmer reported that one of his sheep had been attacked by what seemed to be a large cat and during October 2010 statements from Darlington described a sheep with its front legs and half its neck eaten.

SIX

SUPERNATURAL SIGHTINGS ON THE INDUSTRIAL FRONT

DARLINGTON has had a prime place in railway history since the opening of the line to Stockton on 27 September 1825 and as the rail network gained rapid momentum County Durham alone saw the opening of seventeen separate railways between 1828 and 1894.

Two stations were opened in Darlington during this period of dramatic growth. North Road Station was built in 1842, while Bank Top, on the main line, became operational in 1887, replacing an earlier station on the same site.

With the reduction of the railway network in 1962, North Road Station was closed and soon began to deteriorate, but the sustained efforts of railway enthusiasts and preservationists saw it reopened as Darlington Railway Centre and Museum. Following a £1.7 million refurbishment project it was re-launched in April 2008 as 'Head of Steam' and, in addition to its range of exhibits and collections, the station has an impressive array of ghostly spectres.

A third-class carriage on the farthest platform at North Road Station was built in 1865 and on several occasions there have been reports of a young girl dressed in Victorian clothing sitting within the carriage. Most of the sightings suggest that she was sitting in the far right compartment at the rear of the carriage. At closing time, members of staff have also heard strange noises coming from the carriage, including the sound of a child singing and laughing, while in 2008, when working late one evening in the waiting room, the museum manager heard loud knocking noises. Making his way across to the carriage, the noises stopped as he peered inside, only to start again once he had returned to his office.

There is no clue as to the identity of the young girl or the man in a red jacket seen by a number of children in the engine compartment of the Tennant 1463 locomotive. On each occasion he is said to have been gazing at the array of controls within the engine of the cab before disappearing. More details are recorded, however, about North Road Station's best-known and scariest ghost …

Just over 150 ago, at around midnight on a cold winter's night, James Durham, the station nightwatchman, decided to head below ground into the porter's cellar to warm himself in front of the fire and to have a bite to eat. The cellar had been part of the railwayman's cottage and still had a fireplace and a gas lamp.

Turning up the gas, he sat on a bench and opened his 'bait tin' only to be startled by the figure of a man emerging from the adjacent coal house.

North Road Station, which opened in 1842.

The intruder was dressed in a 'cut-away coat with gilt buttons, a stand-up collar and a scotch cap' and close behind came a large black retriever dog. Saying nothing, the ghostly stranger strolled casually towards the fire before suddenly turning to raise a fist and land a punch on nightwatchman Durham.

Startled into action, James Durham leapt to his feet and aimed a blow at the phantom figure only for his fist to pass through the assailant's body and bruise his knuckles on the stonework of the fireplace surround. With a loud shriek the intruder reeled backwards and at the same moment the snarling dog bit into Durham's leg. Within seconds the confrontation was over and, as James reached for his lantern, the man and his dog turned back into the coal house and disappeared from view. There was no other point of entry or exit but the nonplussed nightwatchman could find no trace of man or dog.

As news of James Durham's ghostly ordeal spread around Darlington, moves were made to verify the authentic nature of his story. Edward Pease, the 'father of the railways', questioned him closely about the incident and, some forty years later in 1890, Revd Henry Kendall, minister of the Congregational church in Darlington, persuaded James to sign a statement about what he had witnessed. With his assertions about the ghostly episode seemingly beyond doubt, Revd Kendall passed his findings to W.T. Stead, a former editor of the *Northern Echo*, and in 1891 he arranged for publication of the railway cellar sighting in a *Census of Hallucinations*, a periodical of the Society for Psychical Research.

It was also discovered during a conversation between Revd Kendall and a former railway employee that long before James Durham had worked at the station a railway clerk had committed suicide by shooting himself with a pistol. Details on the death certificate of Thomas Munro Winter verified his actions on Thursday, 6 February 1845.

In more recent times there have been reports that the ghost of Thomas Winter continues to make an appearance. During a winter evening in the early 1950s the ticket clerk was at his counter in the station booking office when the last train of the day pulled into the platform. He heard the clear sound of a carriage door open and a passenger stepping down before slamming the door shut. The sound of footsteps crossing the platform followed but as the clerk waited … there was no passenger. He left the ticket office to seek out the mystery passenger but the station was completely empty and from end to end of the platform the covering of snow was undisturbed.

During the 1970s, when the station platform was in a neglected state, a visitor to the museum reported that her boyfriend saw the figure of a man and his dog walking over the footbridge. The figure was observed making his way up one set of steps and across the upper section of the bridge before vanishing into thin air as he came down the final section of the stairway.

Of the Darlington district's many ghostly episodes this is probably the best known and most often reported. Within the museum area the cellar entrance is now bricked up but a glass panel allows a view of the room where nightwatchman James Durham came across an uninvited visitor and his loyal dog.

Phantom Figure on the Night Shift

In July 1970 Darlington's *Evening Dispatch* reported on an unscheduled interruption to the night shift operations at the town's Darlington and Simpson Rolling Mills. The walk out by the eight-man workforce at the company, which had twice won the 'Queen's Award to Industry', was not over pay, redundancies or problems with machinery but because of the antics of a ghost.

Imagine the workers' feelings of consternation, then disbelief, as they caught sight of a phantom figure in the company's finishing mills. As they downed tools and walked towards it, the eerie shape reportedly vanished through the wall of the building. While there was generally a reluctance to speak about the incident, witness accounts indicated that the ghost had waved its arms around and moaned as workers moved towards it before disappearing after one man threw a stone at it.

About a dozen men made their way into the roadway in search of the apparition and saw it balancing on top of another nearby wall. It was on top of this wall that an energetic young steel worker used to entertain his mates with acrobatic feats during tea breaks … until one day he fell off the wall and broke his leg.

Sadly, the young worker and four of his colleagues were killed in an accident during the 1920s when an overhead-cable railway crashed and stories of an appearance by 'a vague grey shape' had persisted since that time.

Operations at the mill, which manufactured large steel sections for export to Europe and Asia, soon returned to normal, though some workers showed a reluctance to go to the end of the mill where the apparition had been seen. Meanwhile, the assistant works manager described the reports of a ghostly presence as 'absolute rubbish' and added '… It's some crank talking' while, in a more light-hearted vein, one of the supervisors commented, '… If it turns up again we can put it to work filing rivets!'

SEVEN

GHOULISH GOINGS-ON AT SCHOOL

SCHOOLDAYS are often cited as 'the happiest days of our lives' but they also probably provide some of the scariest moments and most people can recall talk of ghostly incidents during their time at school.

Darlington is no exception and perhaps the best known is a spectral presence in the town's Carmel Technical College. Formed in September 1974 by the amalgamation of St Mary's Boys Secondary School and the Immaculate Conception Secondary School for Girls, the site formerly belonged to the Pease family and their country house home now forms part of the administration block. It dates from 1864 and its rooms, corridors and precincts are said to be haunted by a ghost with the name of Harriet. Her favourite paranormal setting is claimed to be the head teacher's office, where she stands with a self-imposed watching brief.

Hummersknott School replaced the town's girls' high school and soon set and maintained extremely high academic and sporting standards. During my four years on the teaching staff in the mid-1970s I cannot claim to have come across any supernatural presence but other reports indicate that 'an intelligent and straight-laced lady' – presumably a former pupil or member of staff – recalled that the sports hall at Hummersknott was haunted by a bouncing basketball.

Paranormal experiences were often a subject of conversation among pupils at Haughton Comprehensive and a recurring spectral presence took the form of a rat in the area around the biology laboratory.

Phantoms at the Forum Music Centre

In recent years one of Darlington's Victorian school buildings has become a vibrant town centre venue for a range of musical events. Officially opened on 5 May 1879 as Brunswick Street Board School, it was renamed Borough Road School in 1915 when, no doubt, much

Forum Music Centre (originally Brunswick Street Board School).

of the conversation would have been about a visit to the school in 1907 by one of England's foremost cricketers, Dr W.G. Grace.

After standing empty for several years following the closure of the school in 1967, the premises became Durham Music School during 1974. Thirty years later the Forum Music Centre was set up and since 2011 it has been operated by Humanities CIC.

It is during these latter years of the building's history that there have been reports of supernatural activity, including mysterious voices, a dark shadowy figure in one of the corridors and a gently swinging door. Such incidents led to the building's inclusion in Darlington's list of ghost-hunting venues and during these sessions, guests have reported 'ghostly breath' and being scratched on the back by an unseen presence.

EIGHT

SUPERNATURAL INCIDENTS AT DURHAM TEES VALLEY AIRPORT

THE RUNWAYS and buildings of Durham Tees Valley Airport spread across land on both sides of the current boundary between Stockton and Darlington districts. Initially it was known as RAF Goosepool, named after the nearby Goosepool Farm, and during 1941 it became one of 200 wartime bomber bases. Pilots of No. 78 Squadron were soon flying Whitleys while No. 76 Squadron flew Halifaxes against targets in Germany and both squadrons supplied

Durham Tees Valley Airport.

75

more than a score of aircraft for the first 1,000 bomber raids on Cologne. In the later stages of the war, 419, 420 and 428 squadrons of the Royal Canadian Air Force flew Wellingtons, Halifaxes and Lancasters against targets in France and Germany.

During the post-war years the aerodrome was used for a range of training exercises, including a pilot training base, and in November 1954 it was the setting for a tragic episode. Whilst practising manoeuvres in his Meteor Jet aircraft, Raymond Norman lost control and was unable to prevent his aircraft slewing across a parking area in front of a section of the former officers' mess.

By a strange coincidence, out of thirty stationary vehicles in front of the building the only one that was damaged was Raymond Norman's own car. The jet then crashed into the west side of the building where only one room suffered damage and again it was the one used by Pilot Norman. He survived the initial impact and was scrambling out of his wrecked aircraft when falling masonry saw him suffer fatal injuries.

Since then, the western end of the building, which was adapted as the airport hotel, has been the setting for any number of supernatural incidents. Often described as the coldest area of the brick-built structure, both staff members and guests have reported the spectral appearances of an airman wearing the sort of flying jacket that was in use during the war years, 1939–45. From time to time guests have also claimed to feel a weight pressing down on them as they lay in bed, as though an unknown presence was sitting on them.

Durham Tees Valley Airport, showing the model plane on the roof.

Durham Tees Valley Airport with the airfield behind.

During the 1980s a stewardess who was staying at the hotel greeted a man that she passed in the corridor with a cheerful 'Hello'. When there was no reply she turned around but there was no one to be seen and she was left with the image of an airman dressed in a leather flying jacket that was no longer worn by RAF personnel.

Another incident saw a female guest waken during the night to see her husband gazing out of the window. In the semi-darkness she became more aware of her surroundings and realised that her husband was actually still beside her in bed and fast asleep. The eerie figure at the bedroom window then vanished without trace.

Speculation suggests that these ghostly sightings may well be the restless spirit of Raymond Norman and there is a general agreement that he is a friendly spectre who has lost his way or is wandering around the hotel looking for something.

Other reports highlight mysterious and unexplained tapping on windows as well as footsteps across snow-covered areas that suddenly come to an end.

Apart from possible links with Pilot Norman, there are suggestions of a connection with the heroic wartime actions of two Canadian flying officers, J. McMullen and Andrew Charles Mynarski.

Flying Officer McMullen was piloting a Lancaster bomber back to his base at Middleton St George on 13 January 1945 when the badly crippled aircraft began to lose height. It soon became obvious that the bomber was not going to reach the airfield and, after ordering the rest of the crew to bale out, McMullen stayed at the controls in order to crash land the aircraft away from built-up areas around Darlington. (McMullen Road in the town was named in his honour after the war.)

Andrew Charles Mynarski was on an overseas mission when his aircraft was hit by enemy fire and the rest of his crew had already baled out when he crawled through burning oil to reach a colleague, Pat Brophy, who was trapped in the rear gunner's section.

Andrew Mynarski's act of heroism earned him the posthumous award of the Victoria Cross, the last VC to be awarded to an airman in the Second World War. During 2005 a statue of Andrew Mynarski was unveiled at Middleton St George, close to the airfield, and on 28 August 2014 the Mynarski Memorial Lancaster paid a visit to Durham Tees Valley Airport. One of only two airworthy Lancasters in the world, it was making a rare visit to the United Kingdom from its base at the Canadian Warplane Heritage Museum to take part in selected stages of the RAF Battle of Britain Flight. Its stay on Teesside turned out to be longer than planned. The aircraft was grounded a day after the dramatic flypast at Durham Tees Valley Airport when an oil leak during a thirty-minute demonstration flight took out the outer starboard engine.

During a five-day stay in a hangar at the airport, engineers worked to replace the engine and, following a successful test flight, the Mynarski Memorial Lancaster was able to leave for its next port of call, RAF Coningsby in Lincolnshire.

More than forty years earlier, on 26 August 1963, one of Britain's best-known female pilots, Diana Barnato Walker MBE, had taken off from Middleton St George in a Lightning aircraft. During her flight she reached a speed of Mach 1.65 (1,262mph), which made her the first British woman to break the sound barrier and at the same time it set a world speed record for women.

Since the 1960s the former wartime aerodrome has been developed as a civil airport with the first scheduled flight to Manchester in 1966. Changes in more recent years include its renaming as Durham Tees Valley Airport in 2004 but reports of ghostly incidents persist …

NINE

SUPERNATURAL LOCATIONS JUST BEYOND DARLINGTON

Hurworth Grange

Set in extensive grounds close to the site of an earlier cottage, Hurworth Grange was completed in 1875 to designs by the eminent Victorian architect Alfred Waterhouse. His detailed plans for the building represented a wedding gift for his nephew, James Edward Backhouse, and the large brick-built

Hurworth Grange.

mansion remained in ownership of the Backhouse family until 1912.

It was then occupied by the Rogerson family and later by members of the Spielman family. During the Second World War, Jewish refugees were accommodated at Hurworth Grange and military equipment was positioned in the adjacent grounds. In 1956 the Brothers Hospitallers of St John of God bought the building and it served as their juniorate school until 1967.

Following its purchase by the parish council, Hurworth Grange was officially opened as a community centre on 20 September 1969 and it has continued in frequent use for a range of activities.

At regular intervals patrons have reported different types of paranormal activity in various parts of the building. These include doors opening and closing on their own, unexplained cold spots and drops in temperature, a voice heard on upper floors (when no one was present), spine-tingling sounds in the cellars and sightings of a 'white lady' and a male apparition named Edward.

During the early weeks of 2005, Anomalous Phenomena Investigations, based at Newcastle-on-Tyne, were awarded exclusive rights to research hauntings at Hurworth Grange. In August 2006 a film crew from BBC North East and Cumbria recorded an investigation by this group.

Another view of Hurworth Grange.

West Auckland

While residents of West Auckland proudly recall their soccer team's success in the inaugural World Cup of 1909, there are echoes of much earlier sporting occasions among the fine buildings that surround the large village green. King Henry VIII is believed to have used the former West Auckland Hall as a hunting lodge during visits to the area.

Now operating as the Manor House Hotel, the building retains sections of stonework from the late sixteenth and

Front view of Manor House Hotel, West Auckland.

Side view (south facing) of Manor House Hotel, West Auckland.

mid-seventeenth centuries and displays replica items of the regalia worn by Henry and several of his wives. There are also reports of a range of unnerving incidents. These include regular sightings of apparitions of a small boy, a monk and a young woman. On other occasions voices have been heard from empty rooms, objects have mysteriously moved and one member of staff was locked in a cupboard.

During August 2013 attention focused on the hotel's dining room, which is said to be haunted by the ghost of Elizabeth Granville, the victim of an unsolved murder. Guests at a 'Murder Mystery Evening' helped to interrogate suspects and money raised at the event was donated to a local charity.

A short distance away a seat beside Darlington Road has been nicknamed 'Mary's seat' by local folk. Provided by West Auckland Parish Council, it is believed to stand on the former site of No. 20 Johnson Terrace (demolished many years ago), which was the home of the infamous murderer Mary Ann Cotton. It was at this address that she poisoned three of her victims.

Since then there have been numerous sightings of writhing ghostly figures behind the seat and local residents have reported a chill in the air surrounding the seat itself.

'Mortham Dobby'

Countryside to the west of Darlington not only offered an escape route for lawbreakers from places in the Tees Valley, but also afforded a transit trail for armies involved in centuries of border warfare. With this background it is perhaps no real surprise to come across some extremely dramatic haunted locations, including Mortham Tower.

On the southern bank of the Tees at Rokeby, some 3 miles south-east of Barnard Castle, stands Mortham Tower. Described as one of the oldest inhabited building in the area, it represented the most southerly border pele towers destroyed by Scottish forces following the Battle of Bannockburn. Rebuilt in the fifteenth century by the Lord of Rokeby, ownership later passed to the Morritt family and it was then that the tower attracted the interest of Sir Walter Scott.

He described it as 'one of the most enviable places I have seen' and requested information from J.B.S. Morritt on aspects of the building's history, including tales of the 'Headless Dobby'. Morritt's correspondence explained that the female ghost was either an heiress of the Rokeby family who was murdered by a greedy rival or a Lady Rokeby, wife of the owner who was shot by robbers while strolling around the estate.

Whatever the apparition's identity, it had the appearance of a finely dressed noble lady with trailing white silk. Although the ghost had no head, long hair trailed from her shoulders and other facial features of eyes, a nose and a mouth were set in her breast.

Mr Morritt also reported that the local parson had managed to confine the apparition for some time under the bridge close to the confluence of the rivers Greta and Tees. However, serious floods during 1771 caused extensive damage to the single-arched bridge and the apparition was released to roam free in the neighbourhood, where it was spotted by local residents.

In more recent times, the *Northern Echo* reported that the owner of Mortham Tower Farm had woken one night to catch sight of a ghostly headless female sitting in the bedroom. As he watched, she raised herself gently before turning sharply and disappearing from view.

On another occasion, a young Irishman lodging in the house claimed that he was unable to sleep because of the sounds of loud music and dancing. Yet the source of the noise remained unexplained.

Mortham Tower, which is a Grade I listed building, is privately owned and not open to members of the public.

Ghosts Galore Among the Glories of Raby Castle

Located at the heart of some 200 acres of attractive parkland, Raby's impressive array of walls, towers and gateways form one of the largest inhabited castles in England. One of the early landowners in these parts was King Cnut and he may well have built a manor house here but it was the Neville family who built the fourteenth-century castle that stands today.

Raby Castle's medieval, Regency and Victorian architecture and interiors represents one of the finest examples in the whole of the country. It is also the setting of any number of ghostly presences.

Perhaps the best known is the apparition of a lean, handsome figure, Charles Neville, 6th Earl. His grave is in Holland but he regularly sweeps through the castle's galleries with hardly a disdainful glance for portraits of the Vanes and Barnards. Raby belonged to his family for centuries before he brought their ownership to a dramatic end, and it was here in the vast Baron's Hall that events unfolded.

Sitting at the head of a huge table in 1569, Charles Neville had planned the Rising of the Northern Earls but the assembled company had voted against it. Neville's wife then stormed into the hall and, calling them cowards and knaves who dared not fight for their faith, she reversed their decision with her forceful words. They fought ... and lost. Charles Neville fled to Scotland and from there to Holland, while his family lost everything. Perhaps it is a remnant of his guilt that causes his spirit to return to this magnificent setting.

Raby Castle.

Another of Raby's ghostly apparitions frequents the library. Crouched at his desk and busy writing, there is something strange about this shadowy figure … indeed, very strange, for his body ends at the shoulders. His head lies on the desk facing him, with the lips moving as if dictating a letter or delivering a speech.

This is Henry Vane the Younger, who spent much of his life embroiled in the turbulence that characterised struggles between king and Parliament in seventeenth-century England. A trumped-up treason charge led to the execution scaffold far away from his beloved Raby, when he was aged 49, and so his spirit returns …

A quite different phantom is said to prowl the corridors and chambers of Raby before emerging on the battlemented ramparts. Quite elderly, yet still fearsome, this female apparition has wild, staring eyes that glow red during the hours of darkness.

Strangely, the first Lady Barnard, or 'Old Hell Cat' as she became known during her lifetime, is always knitting with white-hot needles. Her fury, it seems, was fuelled by the actions of her sons William and Gilbert, who had reached adulthood and were making their own decisions on important matters.

In particular, Lady Barnard took strong exception to Gilbert's choice of wife. So vehement was her objection to his marriage to Mary Randyll that she and Lord Barnard ruled that their sons would not inherit Raby. Old Hell Cat's rage soon reached extreme proportions as she stripped the castle of furniture, lead and glass. Oak floors were pulled up, trees cut down and the herd of deer was culled as she took her displeasure out on everything in reach.

The epic family fall-out reached a climax when Gilbert took his parents to court. They were ordered to restore the castle to its original condition … at considerable cost … and Lady Barnard's continuing rage accounts for her eerie apparition, which is still said to appear above the dark outline of Raby Castle's ramparts.

Old Spirits in a New Town

The initial phase of Newton Aycliffe's development was marked by the establishment of a munitions factory during the early stages of the Second World War. This location, on the west side of the A167 and just a few miles to the north of Darlington, was noted for the number of days when fog and cloud might offer cover from enemy aircraft … and this may have a bearing on the number of ghostly sighting reported in the area.

Some persistent reports include little detail and refer only to the apparition of a lady in a white dress spotted on the roadside near the Gretna Green Hotel. At other times the sighting has been linked to the discovery of a woman's body in the nearby River Skerne during 1698 and the clothing is identified as a wedding dress and veil.

A rather different apparition is said to haunt a section of railway track between Greenfield Community College and Newton Aycliffe Station. This line linked the pioneering locomotive works at Shildon with Darlington and, during the early days of steam, a man on horseback and carrying a red flag rode ahead of the train. He also carried a bell to sound a warning to cattle or unwary pedestrians who might have wandered on to the track. The spectre at this location is said

Newton Aycliffe Railway Station.

to be one of the bell men who fell from his horse and struck his head on the tracks (after his mount had been startled by the locomotive). Although no such incident is recorded in railway annals, reports in recent times indicate the sounds of a horse neighing and striking its hooves in terror while a bell is heard ringing in the background.

Newton Aycliffe has several care homes for the elderly and one in particular has been the setting for regular reports of supernatural activity. The building in question covers two floors, with recreation and social rooms, laundry and a dining room on the ground floor and residents' rooms as well as a smaller social room on the first floor. A long corridor led to this small social room and it was in this part of the building that most sightings have been reported.

On one occasion members of staff spotted an elderly male resident standing in the doorway at the entrance to the social room. They were convinced that the gentleman had got out of bed but by the time they reached the social room it was empty. He had not passed them on the corridor and the only other exit from the room, via a fire door, remained locked.

At other times two women were in the room when they noticed a white misty shape spreading towards them and understandably made a hasty retreat. Members of staff also reported furniture in the social room moving around as if propelled by an unseen hand and, after a plant pot inexplicably slid off the windowsill and broke on the floor, staff who fetched cleaning items found that the soil had formed a curious crescent moon shape.

Most of the domestic and industrial buildings at Newton Aycliffe have been constructed on agricultural land, but local householders have still reported sightings of past spirits. These include the owner of a property in Mellanby Crescent who stated that on several occasions he and his wife spotted a male figure dressed in riding boots, a dark cape and a red shirt.

Thames Shopping Centre, Newton Aycliffe.

Lake at West Park, Newton Aycliffe.

St Clare's church, Newton Aycliffe.

TEN

GHOST HUNTING IN TIMES PAST

UNTIL late Victorian times it was widely believed in northern England that on St Mark's Eve (24 April) the spirits of people who would die during the following twelve months would haunt churchyards between 11 p.m. and 1 a.m. before entering the church building itself.

Older mensfolk used to gather in church porches to keep a morbid watch and some reports suggest that the watchers must be fasting or must complete a circle around the church before taking up their position.

The ghosts of those who were to die soonest would be the first to emerge while those who would see out the year would not appear until about 1 a.m. Other more gruesome variations of this superstition stated that the watchers would see headless or rotting corpses or possibly coffins approaching the churchyard.

Another widely held tradition in northern parts maintained that a young woman could see the face of her future husband in the fabric of her smock by holding it in front of the fire on St Mark's Eve.

The subject of the paranormal continues to fascinate and intrigue many people from very different walks of life. While scientific and academic research into such matters are pursued by university departments and well-established institutions, ghost hunts, supernatural investigations and similar ventures are arranged in many towns and cities throughout the country.

More than fifty years ago, in 1960, G.W. Lambert completed a survey into London's lost (i.e. underground) rivers and reached the conclusion that approximately three quarters of the city's paranormal activity takes place near buried waters. Water is often said to have spiritual properties but sceptics would probably counter Lambert's claims by maintaining that the flow of buried water could be responsible for any strange sound effects.

A very different study, completed in the latter part of 2011, found that near-death experiences are not paranormal but triggered by a change in normal brain function.

Psychologists based at Edinburgh University reviewed a range of phenomena such as out-of-body experiences, visions of tunnels of light or encounters with dead relatives and concluded that they are tricks of the mind rather than a glimpse of the afterlife. In many cases these sensations could be caused by the brain's attempt to make sense of unusual sensations during a traumatic event.

The spread of modern communications systems, primarily the Internet, has facilitated discussion and debate on supernatural matters, display of images and organisation of a range of ghost hunts, tours or investigations. Many have a commercial element while the social aspect features prominently with such groups.

During the winter of 2006, members of the Darlington Ghost Watch Group recounted their experiences during investigations at local haunted settings. At times there were unnerving moments when they were pushed, prodded or had their hair pulled, but, for the most part, their encounters were of a pleasant nature.

A range of techniques and approaches were used by watchers to investigate and identify ghostly action. In addition to making use of their own senses, another tried and tested technique involved glass divination using a small glass tumbler with anything up to four people placing their index fingers on top. Questions were asked of any resident spirits and movement of the glass meant a positive response while a halt in movement indicated a negative. Unlike an Ouija board there were no letters involved in the exercise. Members made conclusions by this method and then had them verified by owners of the building … much to their own amazement.

Another method involved the use of dowsing rods in determining whether a paranormal presence was male or female and the circumstances of death, i.e. murder or accident. (This method indicated that the spirit in room 16 at Walworth Castle was murdered in the fifteenth century.)

Other items of equipment used by Darlington Ghost Watchers included night vision cameras, which have enabled them to spot orbs and figures. At Walworth, members of the group observed part of a figure moving towards them during such an exercise in room 16. Sightings of ghostly figures were also made in this way at the Otter and Fish Inn at Hurworth. The group similarly used an electromagnetic field meter, thermometer and voice recorder that picked up the sound of ghostly voices in dungeons at Walworth, including a female voice saying 'please help' and an old man asking 'who's that?' Lots of recordings included mainly background noise so it was a considerable surprise to hear the distinct voices.

Photographic evidence also revealed orbs (glowing spheres) and strange mists as well as a single figure in one print.

Drawing conclusions from their observations, members of the group suggested that the spirits were unable to rest due to unfinished business or because they were trapped. Some of the spectres perhaps wanted to stay near loved ones or return to a place that they were particularly fond of.

EPILOGUE

SCEPTICS or cynics may well point to centuries of supernatural sightings with no definite proof of the existence of ghosts, but a study by the Association for the Scientific Study of Anomalous Phenomena concluded in 2013 that belief in ghosts is increasing in the United Kingdom.

Over half of the people that took part in the survey (52 per cent) confirmed that they believed in supernatural occurrences. This represented a considerable increase on the two previous similar studies, undertaken in 2009 and 2005, which indicated that about 40 per cent supported the existence of ghosts. The most recent study also revealed that one in five people claimed to have experienced some kind of paranormal experience.

The chairman of the organisation behind the survey, Dave Wood, expressed surprise at the increase. 'It could be,' he explained, 'that in a society which has seen uncertainty and is dominated by information and technology, more people are seeking refuge in the paranormal, whereas in the past they might have sought that in religion.'

Although belief in ghosts is increasing, the study of more than 2,000 people indicated a fall in the numbers prepared to accept the existence of UFOs. A figure of 52 per cent in 2008 had fallen five years later to 39 per cent. Dave Wood's concluding remark was that belief in UFOs had been declining for some time while a belief in ghosts remained easier to sustain.

Interest in the supernatural has certainly become big business, as indicated by the popularity of television shows such as *Most Haunted* and the increasing number of organised 'ghost walks' around city and town centres. English Heritage and the National Trust have also begun to attract more people to their sites by identifying those said to be occupied by ghosts.

As interest in ghost hunting grows it should be remembered that health and safety aspects, along with legal aspects such as trespass, must always remain paramount.

During May 2013 a charity ghost hunt planned for the workingmen's club in Cockfield, near Bishop Auckland, had to be abandoned when the club committee ruled that the event could not go ahead on health and safety grounds. Happily, the event was rearranged to take place in the former Marquis of Granby pub in Byers Green, which had been empty for some time.

The owner of the property, which had been renamed Thomas Wright House after the famous astronomer from Byers Green, recalled the conversion work that had taken place a few years earlier. As one of the workers removed an internal wall, a fireplace was uncovered and he was amazed to see a female apparition step out. At this point the workman fled and refused to return to the building.

The charity ghost hunt took place during mid-June 2013 and, along with proceeds from another event, almost £850 was raised. This money was split between The Oaks Secondary School, Spennymoor, and Newcastle's Royal Victoria Infirmary.

During April 2014, police officers issued a warning about the dangers facing trespassers at the former St Peter's School on the outskirts of Gainford. The large red-brick building was completed in 1900 as an orphanage for 300 boys, it then served as a school and, most recently, as a nursing home before standing empty since 1997. The officers described rumours on social media about sightings of ghosts at the site as 'total rubbish' and warned that people found on the site would be arrested.

Some places – towns, cities and villages – certainly seem to have many of the features and settings that would be associated with supernatural incidents and the Darlington area fits readily into this category. Its closeness to the waters of the rivers Skerne and Tees, as well as Baydale Beck, a whole series of parks, green spaces and woodland routes, provides a range of outdoor settings, while an assortment of fascinating buildings, from coaching inns to fine Victorian mansions, are all perfect for ghostly goings-on.

Although I cannot claim to have witnessed supernatural activity in the Darlington area, many people have made such assertions. A number of cases can be readily assigned to the realms of folklore, while others may well be the product of an emotional state of mind at a time of crisis or tragedy; additionally some undoubtedly result from the inebriated condition of spectators.

Enough incidents and examples remain to warrant serious consideration, however, and there can be little doubt that the subject opens up a whole new perspective on areas of local life. I hope you will enjoy investigating these haunted sites for yourselves, if you dare …

ABOUT THE AUTHOR

ROBERT WOODHOUSE was a teacher for over thirty years and currently lectures on aspects of local history and tutors courses for adults on the heritage of north-east England. He is the author of thirty-five books on regional history, and lives in Middlesbrough.

SELECT BIBLIOGRAPHY

Newspapers

Darlington and Stockton Times
Evening Dispatch
Northern Dispatch
Northern Echo

Magazines and Local Business Leaflets

Darlington Drinker, Issue 184 (Summer 2012)
North Magazine, Volume 1, No. 2 (August 1971)
North Magazine, Volume 6 (December 1971) – with reference to 'A Modern Ghost Story – A Kind of Revenge'
The History of Blackwell Grange

Books

Dane, Rebecca and Craig MacNeale, *Further Tales of Phantoms Fear and Fantasy Around the North* (Nordales, 1976)
Hallam, Jack, *Ghosts of the North* (David & Charles, 1976)
Woodhouse, Robert, *Supernatural Cleveland and District* (Printability Publishing Limited, 1996)

Websites

www.mysteriousbritain.co.uk
www.paranormalhistory.webs.com

Also from The History Press

More Spooky Books

Find these titles and more at
www.thehistorypress.co.uk

The History Press

Also from The History Press

GRIM ALMANAC

The *Grim Almanac* series is a day-by-day catalogue of ghastly tales from history. Full of dreadful deeds, macabre deaths and bizarre tragedies, each almanac includes captivatingly diverse tales of highwaymen, smugglers, murderers, bodysnatchers, duellists, poachers, witches, rioters and rebels, as well as accounts of old lock-ups, prisons, bridewells and punishments. All these, plus tales of accidents by land, sea and air, and much more, are here. If you have ever wondered about the nasty goings-on of yesteryear, then look no further – it's all here. But do you have the stomach for it?

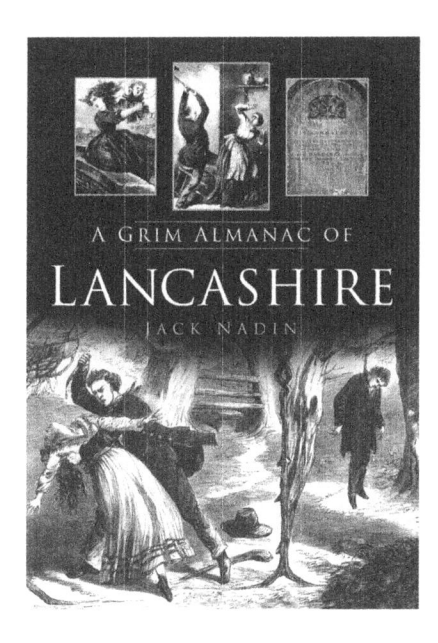

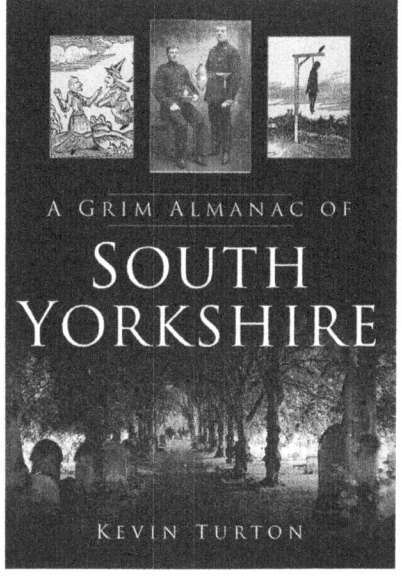

Find these titles and more at
www.thehistorypress.co.uk